Taking the Heat

Vladimir looked into Danko's face and snapped his fingers. Nikolai dropped the white-hot stone into Danko's hand. As the heated stone hit Danko's skin, pain shot through his body. The flesh seared and burned, the intense agony seized his hand like a red-hot iron glove. As he fought with the desire to scream, he brought his fist slowly up to his chin. His knuckles were as white as the stone itself as he applied more and more pressure, crushing the heat from the pebble.

In spite of himself, Vladimir stared in awe. Danko hadn't uttered a sound. In his bones, Vladimir began to get worried—then scared.

RED HEAT

A novel by Robert Tine based on a screenplay by
Harry Kleiner & Walter Hill and Troy Kennedy Martin

AVON BOOKS ◆ NEW YORK

RED HEAT is an original publication of Avon Books. This work has never before appeared in book form. This work is a novel. Any similiarity to actual persons or events is purely coincidental.

AVON BOOKS
A division of
The Hearst Corporation
105 Madison Avenue
New York, New York 10016

Copyright © 1988 by Carolco Pictures, Inc.
Published by arrangement with Carolco Pictures, Inc.
Library of Congress Catalog Card Number: 87-91843
ISBN: 0-380-75565-3

First Avon Books Printing: June 1988

AVON TRADEMARK REG. U.S. PAT. OFF. AND IN OTHER COUNTRIES, MARCA REGISTRADA, HECHO EN U.S.A.

Printed in the U.S.A.

K–R 10 9 8 7 6 5 4 3 2 1

Chapter One

The two officers of the Moscow militia, Ivan Danko and his partner Yuri Ogarkov, stepped out of the cold, snowy Moscow street and into a dilapidated building in an old part of Moscow on the Potemkim Prospekt. It was a street once proud and prosperous, now grown shabby and run-down through years of war and neglect. The building housed gymnasium—old, prerevolution Danko thought, and brought to mind Lenin's famous dictum: that the world would be remade through fire and iron.

More than anything else, the gym was a world of fire and iron. In the huge exercise room, the air damp and hot, a miasma of steam and sweat, giant muscular men, and women of equal—in some cases greater—stature, groaned and strained against ancient weight machines. Their muscles rippled as they worked against great hunks of cast iron, pumping huge barbells and letting them fall with a juddering crash to the worn wood floor. It seemed as if the room were wrapped in iron. Thick old steam pipes snaked along the walls and across the ceiling, rattling with hot water and steam, feeding the old riveted tubs of water in which heavyweight lifters, men and women alike, soaked in the scalding water like reptiles in a swamp pool. Valves hissed and smoked as the pipes carried hot water and steam to the saunas beyond the main weight room. A world of fire and iron, Danko thought again.

The two cops surrendered their clothes to the ancient attendant at the door, the old man scarcely noticing as Danko stripped off his shirt to reveal a powerful, muscular body, castellated with muscles. Strong, hard men were not uncommon there. Yuri, slighter, less muscular than his companion, slung a towel around his neck. He was a strong man, a dangerous man in a fight, but next to Danko and the other mountainous creatures in the gym he looked puny.

As the two policemen stepped into the weight room, an antique copper-riveted boiler grumbled like thunder presaging a violent storm. Steam belched from the loose joints. A stoker, his face ham-pink and streaked with coal dust and sweat, looked up from his boiler and stared at Yuri and Ivan. He held a piece of iron, a poker probably, in one huge fist. He shook it menacingly. He knew cops when he saw them— and they weren't welcome there.

Danko stared through him. "They're here," he said to Yuri. "I can smell them."

Yuri nodded. He looked from body to body,

searching the crowd for Viktor and his band of thugs. "In the steam room?"

Danko nodded and walked toward a door on the far side of the room. He passed a giant, naked, Olympian figure who was straining to keep a three-hundred-pound weight lifted high above his head. As Danko drew level with him, he lost his unequal struggle, letting the barbell crash to the floor in Danko's path. He did not flinch, stepping over it.

As the two policemen entered the steam room, a splash of hot water hit the white hot pebbles standing in a blistering brazier in the middle of the room. Steam rose up, thick and wet, enveloping the stifling room. It was like walking into thick cloud cover. Through the steam, Danko could make out the figures of men and women lazing on the smooth pine benches. They stared expectantly into the steam, looking at Danko's powerful form with interest, like theater spectators waiting for the curtain to go up on the first act.

"Cops," said one of the men matter of factly. Danko glanced at him. He knew the face from the dossier on Viktor and his gang. That was Nikolai, a drug pedlar, a murderer, a thief, a hooligan. Probably a pimp too. Danko and Yuri would take great pleasure in bringing him in. But that was for later. Right now they were after bigger game.

"He says you are police," said another man through the haze. Danko looked. This was Vladimir, known as The Hippy. He had a wide, almost Oriental face and shoulders broad enough to support a bus. His thick black hair was long and shaggy. Rolls of flesh coiled around his thick, flabby neck. Buried in the greasy folds were silver and gold chains.

"I said, 'He says you are from the militia.' "

"I am a foundry worker," said Danko. "From Kirov."

The Hippy smiled a wide, thick-lipped smile. "You're a long way from home." He lumbered over to Danko, and seized the policeman's hand, examining it as if he were a doctor. "This is not the hand of a foundry worker."

"Idi na huy," growled Danko. Go fuck yourself.

The fat man's face darkened. "We'll see what you really are. A little test, to see if you really work in a steel foundry."

The men and women on the benches leaned forward, gazing through the steam. This would be interesting.

"Nikolai," barked The Hippy. "Warm up our friend from Kirov."

Nikolai grinned. He picked up a pair of iron tongs and selected a single burning pebble from the brazier, choosing the coal with all the care of a child choosing a sweet from a box. He held the little stone almost daintily in the tongs. He brought it to Danko, holding it above Ivan's still outstretched hand.

The tough cop never took his eyes off Vladimir's smirking face. Danko knew what was coming, was bracing himself for the pain, silently determined to show no emotion. He channeled his hate into his eyes, staring hard at Vladimir, as if deriving strength from his intense loathing of the man.

Vladimir, with a sadist's precision, squared off Danko's palm, pulling the fingers straight. "Ni bzdi," he said with a giggle. Now don't be a coward. He spoke as if to a child about to have an injection. "If you work in a foundry you will be used to the heat. This will be nothing at all."

He looked into Danko's face and snapped his fingers. Nikolai sneered and dropped the white-hot pebble into Danko's hand.

As the heated stone hit the skin of Danko's hand, pain shot through his body. The flesh seared and burnt, the intense agony seized his hand like a red-hot iron glove. A strange silence filled the room as Danko's eyes blazed, his mouth twisted, his teeth clamped together like a vise. The sounds of the gym seemed to recede as he wrestled with the pain. He said nothing.

Danko closed his fingers, making his hand into a huge fist. He squeezed his fingers down hard into the palm of his hand, locking them there with his thumb. It was as if he were trying to wring the heat from the stone and the pain from his hand. As he fought with the intense desire to scream, he brought his fist slowly up to his chin and held it there, as if filling the space between him and Vladimir. His knuckles were as white as the stone itself as he applied more and more pressure, crushing the hot pain from the pebble.

In spite of himself, Vladimir stared, awed and scared. The cop hadn't uttered a sound. In his bones, Vladimir began to get worried—then scared.

Pain and hatred fused in an explosive, potent mix in Danko's brain. Then it ignited, blasting into his muscles like a hot, fiery liquid. At the bursting point, his giant fist lashed out, blistering across Vladimir's chin. The power of the blow seemed to rip his beard away, as if it were false, then blasted him against the flimsy pine walls of the steam room. All three hundred pounds of the gangster pounded into, then through, the wooden wall. The steam room was suddenly suffused in a bright, white, snow-driven light.

Vladimir screamed as his hot flesh hit the subzero temperatures of the outside. He was floundering on the tiny balcony beyond the steam room, his callused feet already chilled to the bone by the deep snow there. But he knew one thing. He wasn't going back in there to face that madman. Naked, freezing, hurt, he threw himself over the railing of the balcony, landing in a few feet of snow twenty feet below.

No sooner had he hit the ground, than Danko was after him. The big cop jumped from the balcony without a second thought, screaming in rage and hate as he launched himself into space.

Vladimir stumbled to his feet and managed to toss Danko over his shoulder as the cop landed on him. As Ivan passed, he got a handful of The Hippy's greasy hair and wrenched it hard, as if he were trying to scalp him. He yanked him to the ground and punched him hard. In Vladimir's mouth a couple of teeth cracked and split. He screamed in pain, an incoherent mass of oaths and threats breaking from his throat.

Vladimir's big fist shot out toward Danko's chin, but it was a slow, ill-aimed blow. Ivan took his enemy's fist in his own and squeezed. A finger snapped. Then Danko put a knee as heavy and as hard as a battering ram in Vladimir's chest. The criminal gasped like a train letting off steam, the air knocked from his lungs. He fell into the snow, Danko dropping himself onto Vladimir's bucking chest, falling on him like a pile driver. He seized Vladimir in a bone-crunching leg-lock, compressing his already damaged chest until The Hippy gasped for breath like a fish out of water. Danko's fist, as hard and as heavy as a load of bricks, cracked into Vladimir's jaw again. The bone gave up its unequal struggle and split like green wood. Vladimir felt his brain seize up like an old engine and his mouth filled with blood. He had had enough.

The moment Danko had punched Vladimir in the steam room, Yuri had swung into action. He planted a sharp elbow in Nikolai's temple, dropping him to the damp floor. As Danko had gone out the hole in the wall after Vladimir, Yuri had found himself dealing with the stoker who had left his boiler to have some fun beating up the two cops who dared to come into the Druzbha. He swung his poker in a murderous, vicious arc, narrowly missing Yuri's head. But the lithe young cop caught the great paw, slammed it against the wall and made the man drop his iron weapon.

But the stoker was strong, and far from finished. He grabbed Yuri by the shoulders and tossed him against the pipe-wrapped wall. But Yuri came off them like a wrestler off the ropes, slamming a hard right into the stoker's face. The blow caught the man unawares, dazing him. Ogarkov got a handful of sweaty hair and slammed the stoker's head against the wall. Slowly, he slid to the floor.

But there was another enemy to deal with. Coming out of the steam was a Tartar, snarling, showing his discolored, broken teeth. A long, lethal knife was clutched in his hand. He was bent low, the knife held away from his body, looking for an opening.

He didn't get one. Yuri whipped a towel into his face, snapping it in the man's eyes, the way boys do in a locker room. As the rough cloth slapped his eyes, blinding him for a second, Yuri saw his chance. He put all his weight into a single kick that slammed into the big man's crotch. He let out a strangled, agonized scream and dropped like newly cut timber.

Yuri elbowed his way past the cowering naked women who had been enjoying the torture of Danko a few moments before, and stepped out onto the balcony. He dropped into the soft snow next to Danko and the fallen Vladimir.

"Viktor?'" he asked.

Danko nudged The Hippy with his toe. "No. That's not him. But he's here." He scooped up a handful of snow to cool his burning hand. "Where is he, Vladimir?"

Vladimir blubbered something, blood and saliva dripping thick and viscous into the pure white snow.

"Can he talk?" asked Yuri, eyeing the broken man dubiously.

"He can talk," said Danko. He kicked the prostrate man savagely. "Where is he, Vladimir? Viktor, where is he?"

Through broken teeth Vladimir managed to say: "Druzhba. Tonight at the Druzhba."

It snowed that night, snowed much harder than usual. Danko was at the wheel of an unmarked Volga police sedan, Yuri sitting next to him. The underpowered car plowed through the snow, leading a small procession of similar unmarked vehicles. The three cars behind Danko's held militiamen, foot soldiers who would take Viktor and his gang into custody—when Danko gave the order. Until Danko told them to move, the cops were under strict instructions to stay out of sight.

Danko peered through the ice-encrusted windshield of the Volga. Up ahead somewhere was Druzhba, one of the lowlife bars in the city of Moscow. It was well known to the underworld as a place where you could lay your hands on drugs, weapons, hard currency, bootleg tapes, even electronic equipment like VCRs and stereos. Druzhba was a recruiting office for thieves: if you needed someone to work on a safe or to climb a drain pipe or to drive a getaway car, you went to Druzhba. It was, Danko thought, very much Viktor Rosta's kind of place.

The police knew about Druzhba too and raided it periodically. But every cop in every police department in the world knows that it doesn't matter how strict the police are, someone is always willing to take a risk: to be a thief. Moscow policemen recognized that people steal and they were never going to be able to put an end to it.

But drugs—and they were becoming increasingly available in Moscow—that was another story. Danko was determined to stop the nascent drug traffic. Kill it now, before it really took hold. Viktor Rosta and his family were the pioneers of the traffic, and Danko wanted them behind bars.

"It's all getting harder," said Yuri, as if reading Danko's thoughts. "Ten years ago—no drugs. Now we have a problem. Another ten years"—he sneezed suddenly—"maybe we are Harlem." He blew his nose. "All that rolling around in the snow," he said miserably. "I think I'm getting a cold."

Danko pulled the car in towards the curb. They were a couple of blocks from the bar. They would walk the rest of the way. The other police cars stopped behind them.

"Surround the building," ordered Danko, "but make sure you are discreet about it. And give me ten minutes before you come in."

"Yes, Comrade Captain," said the sergeant who lead the detail.

Yuri and Danko started down the block. Yuri sneezed again.

"My mother taught me a home remedy for colds," said Danko. "It never fails."

Yuri looked hopeful. "Really? What is it?"

"Try holding a hot rock in your hand till your partner shows up."

Yuri laughed. "You're trying to make me believe that little pebble hurt your hand. I don't believe it."

Danko stopped and looked at the bar, then over at Yuri. "You know what to do?"

"Of course. Same routine as usual. You go in the front, I'll wait out back. If you come out the front door with Rosta, well and good. If he tries to go out the back door, I've got him. Simple."

"Good." Danko walked the last few yards to Druzhba—he could hear muffled rock music pounding inside.

He pushed open the door: a wave of music, acrid cigarette smoke, and vodka fumes broke over him. The dark bar was filled with tough-looking characters. They sat at old iron-legged tables, hunched over their drinks and whispering conspiratorially. Danko wondered how many crimes were being planned that snowy night.

The bartender was the first to spot Danko. He knew at once he was a cop—the bartender had seen plenty of them in his career—and he knew immediately that there was going to be trouble. The look on Danko's face told him that this particular militiaman was not coming in for a quick drink to keep out the cold or even for a bribe. This massive cop meant business. Quickly, the bartender poured himself a drink and swilled it down.

None of the patrons at the bar noticed the bartender's sudden nervousness, and they didn't

notice Danko until he had walked over and
held his ID card under the bartender's nose.

"Danko," he said, "militia."

The men at the bar fell silent, each of them
hoping that this Danko wasn't looking for them.
The other patrons in the smoky tavern were
beginning to take notice of the cop. Gradually
conversation in the room died down.

"I'm looking for Viktor Rosta."

The bartender gulped nervously and glanced
towards the rear of the dark room. Viktor was
a very bad man—he didn't like it when people
informed on him. But, then again, the cop didn't
look like he enjoyed the noncooperation of comrade citizens.

"Against the back wall," said the tavern
keeper in a low voice, "under the window."

Danko nodded and turned. The only sound
now was the Slavic heavy-metal that blasted
out of some old speakers. Danko walked to the
back of the room and stood in front of Viktor.
He was sitting at a table with his brother, a
couple of thugs, and two painted whores.

"Let's go," said Danko. "All of you."

The women, their faces overpainted with lip
stick and makeup, glanced nervously at their
men. Two of Viktor's goons, Yegor and Sasha,
watched Danko closely, ready for—anticipating,
perhaps even savoring—the violence they were
sure was about to erupt. Only the two Rosta
brothers—Viktor, the leader, and Vagran, his
lieutenant—looked as cool and composed as
Danko and Ogarkov. They glanced at the militiaman, apparently uninterested and almost
bored, mirror images of the cool-headed offi-

cers. Danko was a professional policeman, the brothers were professional criminals. It was not the first time they had dealt with the police, it would not be their last.

Viktor, in contrast to the other men in the room, was well dressed, confident that money and menace would always see him through the toughest situations. His suit and shoes were Italian and expensive. Unlike the others he had a glass of expensive Western scotch before him.

Viktor ran his hand through the stubble on his cheeks. He cultivated it carefully, making sure it never burst into a full-fledged beard, yet he never shaved himself down to the skin. It was the look affected by the male fashion models in the expensive Western magazines he read: *Uomo, Vogue, GQ, Interview* . . . He toyed with a small ruby ring on his finger. He wondered which would serve him better—to buy this cop, or kill him.

"Viktor Rosta," said Danko slowly. Even with his powers of self-control, Ivan Danko could not help but let a touch of satisfaction creep into his voice. "I have been looking for you."

Yegor, Sasha, Vagran, the women, all of them looked to Ivan and Viktor. They could feel the power of the two men, each of them hate-filled but calm; they were like powerful magnets, their fields of force emanating, repelling.

"I'm not hard to find," said Viktor, his voice light, amused.

Danko shook his head. "No, I just followed the cocaine and the corpses."

Viktor glanced around the room, smirking at his friends, as if trying to enlist their support to fight off what he considered a gross libel.

"Cocaine? Corpses?" he said in a sham of innocence. "I know nothing about either. Perhaps you have me confused with someone else. Cocaine is the scourge of the decadent West. I have read about it in *Pravda*."

"And you and your brother here sell it to Russians."

"Gavno!" said Vagran, Viktor's brother. Bullshit.

Viktor's reply was a little smoother. His voice was shot through with the tone of aggrieved innocence. "You think my brother and I are for decay of the glorious Motherland?" He spoke as if he couldn't believe his ears.

"You profit from it," said Danko shortly. He had had enough of fencing with this hoodlum. "Let's go," he ordered. "On your feet. All of you."

Viktor's thugs glanced nervously at their boss. His brother looked to him, as if for guidance. The whores had gone pale under their garish makeup.

Wearily, Viktor got to his feet. "Why is it, Comrade Policeman, that you always pick on us poor countryfolk?" He fingered the sleeve of his silk Armani jacket. "We're poor peasants who don't know the ways of the big city. Perhaps that is why we are such easy targets."

It had taken Danko six months to track down Viktor. Men, good men, had been killed. Viktor Rosta and his brother and his scummy gang were not easy targets. They were killers who had to be eliminated. But now the long chase was over. Viktor would now taste some harsh justice. His fancy Western clothes would not be too comfortable where he was going. Danko reached over and snapped off the music. And there wasn't a lot of Scotch whiskey in a Soviet jail.

"Time to go, Viktor."

Viktor sighed, shrugged, and then sprang into action. He threw himself to one side of the room. "Now, Yegor!" he yelled.

Yegor jumped to his feet, yanking a heavy piece of artillery from the wide sleeve of his jacket. The 7.62 automatic roared twice, two heavy slugs gouging out a piece of the door frame near Danko's head. His fire was returned with deadly accuracy. Danko fired three times in a single second, the steel-jacketed 9mm bullets ripping into Yegor's chest, throwing him back, torn, bloody, dead, against the grimy plaster walls.

The women were on their feet, screaming. Glass shattered. The room filled with the acidic smell of burnt gunpowder. Blood from Yegor's chest splashed onto the threadbare carpet.

Danko had his gun up and ready. He took careful aim on Viktor, ready to blow him away with a single, well-placed shot. But one of the women got in his way. He threw her roughly to one side, squeezing off a single round as Viktor and his brother dashed through a side door, splinters from the frame scattering around them.

The old building that housed Druzhba was a warren of staircases and corridors and rooms where the local whores serviced their clients. The barroom was chaos. People were fleeing out of the front door or diving for cover. In the melee, Viktor and his gang managed to dash into the rooms beyond the bar, hoping to lose—or kill—Danko in the labyrinth beyond.

Danko didn't think. He reacted. He crashed through the door, expecting blistering, high-caliber fire. Instead, a bottle of vodka, thrown from the gloom of the long corridor, smashed against the wall above his head. The pungent fumes filled the dark space.

Danko moved stealthily down an eerily silent corridor, his gun held out in front of him. The light was not good. He hugged the walls, ready to blow away anything in his path. Swiftly, silently, he moved along the narrow hallway, his nerves tingling, every part of his body alive and tensed.

He saw the muzzle flash before he heard the sound, heard the explosion of the weapon before he registered the outline of the body firing it. At the end of the hall, in the half-light of a low-wattage bulb stood a figure, combat stance, the large gun in his hand blazing. Four heavy slugs gouged the plaster in the wall next to Danko, as if it had been hit with the claw of a weighty hammer. Ivan couldn't tell if his attacker was Viktor or Vagran—he didn't care, he'd take either. His 9mm roared, firing at the elusive target.

But he was gone.

Ivan Danko could hear footsteps on the wooden floor. They were moving quickly, running. Danko took off, dashing down the remaining yards, like a hunter in full blood after his prey.

Danko listened. The footsteps were irregular, awkward. A heavy footfall followed by a weaker one. It was as distinctive as a man's signature. Ivan knew exactly who he was following.

The corridor lead to a small staircase, a few steps up to another anonymous wooden door that gave no hint of what lay beyond. He crashed through.

He was in a shabby bedroom. A balding fat man and an equally unattractive prostitute were huddled in a corner, scared to death. Their little transaction had suddenly been interrupted by two heavily armed men desperately intent on killing each other. The client whimpered, but the hooker pointed toward some heavily curtained windows. The curtains were blowing, cold air streamed into the room. Danko's gun roared. Two huge holes appeared in the curtains.

Vagran appeared in the window, sweeping the curtains back, his gun blazing. The two women screamed. Danko hit the floor, rolled and came up firing, the detonation of his big gun echoing, ringing in the confined space. Three big slugs tore into Vagran's chest, close grouped, one above his heart, one below and a single one striking it unerringly in its center. The first two shots would have killed Vagran in a matter of minutes. The third one killed him in less than a second. The hopelessly damaged heart stopped midbeat. The gangster toppled into the room, his chest looking like the target of a Class-A shooting student at the Police Training School. Except for the blood.

Danko felt the tight muscles in his back uncoil. He stood up, shook himself, and let the gun drop to his side. He pulled Vagran into the center of the room, and without a glance at the keening man and women sat down on the hoodlum's back. He grabbed Vagran's left leg in his hand and wrenched it back, snapping it off at the knee cap.

The hooker and the client stared, their terrified eyes growing wide. As Danko cracked the leg and pulled it from under the dead man's pant, the woman rolled over and wretched miserably onto the wooden floor. The man fainted dead away.

Danko held Vagran's artificial leg up to the light, as if it were a trophy. Then he tipped it toward the floor. A fine white powder dribbled out like late winter snow. It swirled and mixed with the gray dust.

"Kokaine," he said.

Then he tossed the leg away, the white powder scattering, and wheeled toward the door, his gun coming back into action. A figure appeared there—Sasha, ready to fire—but not quick enough. The gun in Danko's hand blasted one more time. A bullet embedded itself in the middle of the man's forehead. He dropped, dead before he hit the floor.

A second later another man appeared. Danko's

finger tightened on the trigger, but he braked in time. His gun was aimed at the head of a patrolman in the Moscow Militia. The young man's mouth went dry and he stared for a moment, bug-eyed, before he could find his voice.

"Comrade Captain," he managed to blurt out. "Please come. Captain Ogarkov"—Danko was already off and running back along the corridor —"has been shot," the militiaman finished, speaking to Danko's retreating back.

When Viktor jumped from the second floor of the building, into a small courtyard at the back of the building, and made for the rusty iron gate that opened onto the street, Yuri was waiting for him. He stepped out of the shadows, his gun level, his manner calm.

"Hold it right there, Viktor," he said. Yuri was elated. Already he could taste the celebratory vodka he would drink with Danko. He would kid his friend, rubbing in the fact that it was he, Yuri, who had caught the big bad Viktor Rosta, while Ivan Danko had been chasing smaller fry. Ivan would pretend to be annoyed and would swear horribly at him . . . but they both knew that it had been a triumph for both of them, that together they had broken Moscow's biggest drug ring. It would be a moment to savor.

Viktor stopped, feeling on the back of his neck the gun aimed at him.

"You're under arrest, my friend," said Yuri.

Slowly Viktor turned and looked at Yuri. He smiled slightly.

Cool bastard, thought the cop. "Drop the gun," he ordered.

Viktor's big automatic fell silently into a cushion of snow. He held out his hands. "Now the handcuffs, yes?"

"Yes," said Yuri with a smile. They weren't so tough when they had lost, he thought. "I think that would be a good idea."

Viktor shot back his cuffs. "Be careful of the shirt. It was made for me in London."

"Of course, comrade."

Viktor's arms were pointed directly at Yuri's chest. Suddenly, as if something were crawling down Viktor's forearm, a gun appeared in his hand. A spring gun, activated by the flexing of a muscle. It appeared as if by magic. It was not very high caliber, but the two bullets it propelled into Yuri's chest were enough to do the damage. He clutched his breast and dropped. Viktor snapped the gun back up his London-tailored sleeve and walked calmly toward the gate. He turned left on the snow-covered street and disappeared.

He reappeared in Chicago, in the United State of America. He had been arrested by the police there after having been picked up on a minor traffic charge. His name had been fed into the FBI computer, which switched it to the Interpol computer in Belgium, which in turn had notified both the Americans and the Soviets that a major international criminal had been apprehended.

The report of Viktor Rosta's arrest had filtered down through the ranks of the Moscow militia until it had reached the desk of Ivan

Danko's immediate superior. He, Major Bondarev, had informed Danko that the most wanted man in Moscow had been arrested in Chicago. Although outwardly unmoved by the news, Danko had felt his heart beat strong in his chest when told of Viktor's arrest.

"You will go to America," said Bondarev, "and bring him home."

"Yes, Comrade Major," said Danko stolidly.

"Normally I wouldn't send a man like you. You may be a fine police officer, Ivan Ivanovitch, but you have too much of your soul invested in this case. It makes a man a little crazy, I think."

"I will follow my orders, Comrade Major."

"Of course." Major Bondarev offered a thick, black cigar to Danko. "Take one," he urged. "A man must have some pleasures."

Danko had taken the cigar, as if out of obligation, rather than desire, but he had enjoyed it. It was a fine, full-leaf Havana, a type of cigar he would not be able to enjoy in the United States.

"You will be there one night only," his superior informed him. "You will fly in, spend the night, collect the prisoner, and return. Do you understand?"

"Perfectly, comrade."

"Good." The major exhaled a great cloud of blue smoke. "I know what this means to you, Ivan."

No you don't, thought Danko. No one knows what a cop goes through when his partner is killed. Danko had spent nights, long cold nights, replaying the scene in his mind. He went over every move he had made, analyzing, criticizing, wondering if he had been at fault. He could not forget that day.

As soon as he had seen the worried, pasty white fearful face of that young militiaman, Danko knew that Yuri had been hurt. He had dashed into the courtyard, dimly registering the fact that snow around his friend's body was stained red where it was close to the wound, pink a few feet away. People, patrons of the Druzhba, policemen, all had crowded around Yuri's body. Danko had pushed them aside and dropped to his knees next to his fallen partner. You didn't have to be an expert to see that Yuri was well on his way to death. His face was pale, his breath shallow and labored, his lips blue and twisted.

Ivan Danko had cradled Yuri in his arms. "Hang on, my friend," he had said hoarsely, "there's an ambulance coming. Tomorrow we'll laugh about this. Please hang on."

Yuri's eyes had been curiously unfocused, but he had recognized the voice and smiled. "Too late, Ivan. I failed." Danko had felt his friend's body tighten. "I had him. I *had* him. But I failed." Had Yuri had more strength he would have pounded his fist in frustration. But it was a struggle for him to even utter his last words. "You go on from here without me. Promise me, promise me that you'll get him."

"I promise," said Danko solemnly.

Yuri had smiled, content. "Good."

Bondarev was saying something and it took a moment to penetrate Danko's grief clogged brain. ". . . naturally, you won't give a hint to the Americans what this man is wanted for.

We may be friends with them—more or less—
these days, but we don't want to wash our
dirty linen in public, if you understand what
I'm saying."

"Of course, Comrade Major." Danko glanced
out the window. It was summer already in
Moscow. Yuri had died in the winter. It seemed
like yesterday that snow had been two feet
deep on the ground.

Bondarev was saying something else. Danko
pulled himself back to the present.

"Rovoshenko, Lieutenant Rovoshenko, will
bring you your ticket, visas, and anything else
you may need. This evening. Expect the lieutenant this evening." Stepanovitch thrust out
his hand. "Good luck, Comrade Captain Danko."

Danko shook his superior officer's hand.
"Thank you, Comrade Major."

Danko, a careful, methodical man, laid out
his clothes, folding them precisely before laying
them in the battered leather suitcase on his
bed. He put his two civilian suits into the case,
one blue, the other an unappetizing shade of
green, smoothing the creases in the pants as
he did so. It was early evening, and, as if to
remind him of the fact, the _peep-peep_ of the
alarm on his steel watch went off just at six
o'clock. He snapped down the stem, cutting off
the alarm. He walked into his down-at-the-
heel living room and took a cover off a birdcage
and fed the brightly colored parakeet within.

Just then the doorbell rang. He opened the
door to Lieutenant Katya Rovoshenko. She was
a blond, severe-looking woman in her forties,

as dedicated to the activities of the Moscow Militia as Danko himself.

"Comrade Captain," she said, "I have brought your orders."

He stood aside, guided her into the kitchen and took a bottle of vodka from the freezer of the creaky refrigerator. She opened her briefcase, slipped on a pair of horn-rimmed glasses and began to read in her cold, clipped voice.

"Your passport," she said, handing over the red-covered booklet. "And your letters of identification and your international permit to transport a prisoner across international frontiers." Danko took the three buff-colored envelopes and hefted them in his hand, as if weighing them.

"You will be met at O'Hare International Airport by a representative of the Chicago Secret Police."

"Name?"

Rovoshenko scanned her notes. "Not included."

Danko nodded. He would find the man when he arrived.

Rovoshenko took another envelope from her briefcase. This one was fatter than the others. "One thousand dollars, in cash. Every penny of which is accountable. If for any reason it proves to be insufficient or if you experience any difficulties whatsoever, you are to contact the Soviet Embassy in Washington. Your contact there is Vice Consul Gregor Moussorsky, aide to Dimitri Stepanovitch."

Danko memorized the names. "Anything else?"

The last envelope slid across the table. "Viktor Rosta's plane ticket. One way." She picked up her vodka and drained it in a gulp. She refilled it and allowed herself one of her small complement of smiles for the day. "Chicago," she said, "town of American gangsters."

"I'm not interested in American gangsters," said Danko. "I'm interested in our Soviet variety."

"You should not take things so personally, if I may say so, Comrade Captain."

"You have forgotten something," said Danko, ignoring her advice.

Lieutenant Rovoshenko frowned. "I have?"

"My international permit to carry arms."

"You will go unarmed. You are not permitted by the American authorities to carry a gun."

Danko nodded. "As they wish," he said, like a good dutiful cop.

The last thing Ivan Danko did before leaving his apartment for the airport was to take his heavy 9mm pistol from his desk drawer. He slipped it into a false bottom in his battered suitcase. The hell with American regulations. He would not face Viktor Rosta without a weapon. And if he couldn't bring him home to Moscow and justice, he would kill him. It was as simple as that.

Chapter Two

In the Chicago Police Department there were two schools of thought concerning Detective Sergeant Art Ridzik. Some of his fellow detectives were of the opinion that Ridzik was a dedicated, heroic officer whose unorthodox methods propelled him from the ranks of the merely good to the truly great. Detectives holding this opinion, and they included Art Ridzik himself, were in the minority. The other school of thought held that Art Ridzik was a crazy son of a bitch, a major fuck-up who should be thrown off the force before someone got seriously hurt. Both schools, however, conceded that there was no better street operator and that working with him was, to say the least, exciting. Ridzik had a way of attracting bullets—it was like he was magnetized or something.

It was a broiling hot summer afternoon on the south side of Chicago, the kind of day when everyone tries to stay indoors, in the cooling vapors of the air-conditioning. Everyone, that is, except for the three cops in an unmarked police unit that pulled up to the broken curb on a dirty, slummy side street. Art Ridzik was slumped in the backseat, hot, bored and greatly taken with the idea of being someplace else.

His immediate superior, Lieutenant Charles Stobbs, an immaculately dressed young man— the hotshot of the department; everyone said he had *Commissioner* written all over him— sat behind the wheel. In the passenger seat was another detective, Tom Gallagher. All three looked at the broken-down tenement they had stopped in front of.

"Your snitch worth a shit?" asked Stobbs.

"Personally?" said Gallagher. "No. He informs on his friends. How can you like a guy like that? He's scum, but that's his job. You might say it's his vocation. But his information is good. Most of the time, anyway."

Stobbs smoothed his perfectly trimmed mustache. "I can't believe the kind of volume he's talkin'. It's been a real buyer's market for the last two months."

"You know," said Ridzik, "we should be doing something instead of sitting here. We're gonna get made as cops in about ten seconds."

Stobbs half turned in his seat. "What makes you say that, Ridzik?" Fucking Ridzik, thought Stobbs, he always thought he knew everything and had no hesitation about telling people.

"Two white guys sitting in a beat-up sedan with a black guy—you, Lieutenant—and the black guy is dressed like he's a subscriber to *GQ*. What do you think people are going to think? That we're a bunch of architects?"

"Shuttup, Art," mumbled Gallagher. He didn't see any point in making Stobbs angry.

"Street grams are one hundred and forty-two bucks. O-Z's are running—"

"We got the new price sheet, Stobbs," said Ridzik, his voice heavy with boredom.

Stobbs ignored him, as did Gallagher. "I know, I know it doesn't make sense," Gallagher said. He felt he had to defend his informer's information. "But I believe him when he says they're bringing in more, a lot more."

"But the market is glutted. Saturated," countered Stobbs.

"Whoa," said Ridzik from the backseat. He sat up straight and peered eagerly out the window. "Attention, funbag patrol. Double bogies at four o'clock." Coming down the street past their car was a very attractive young woman. Ridzik didn't focus on her face, though, but on her large breasts, which the stretched-tight cloth of a skimpy halter top was not doing much to conceal. The fact that she wasn't topless altogether seemed to be by accident rather than design.

"All right, Ridzik. Cool it. Let's get moving before you faint or something."

"You think she bought those?" asked Ridzik. "I don't think so. I think she grew them at home."

"Art," groaned Gallagher.

Ridzik smiled. "Everyone's entitled to an opinion."

"You're not here for your opinions," said Stobbs, getting out of the car.

Art Ridzik shot one more longing glance at the woman. "I'm a man," he said. "I have needs."

The front door of the tenement was not locked. In the cramped lobby the three detectives stopped and looked warily up the dilapidated stairs. From a floor above them they could hear a TV broadcasting a Cubs game. The stairwell was dark and definitely not inviting.

"You sure your man is good?"

"Yeah," said Gallagher.

"What did you squeeze him with?" asked Ridzik. The girl on the street was forgotten.

"Caught him packin'. He's on parole. I gave him a choice: whisper in my ear or his parole officer is going to find out about the gun he was carrying."

"Which means three-to-five with Miss Joliet," filled in Ridzik.

"Instead, he tipped to this big Cleanhead deal," said Stobbs.

Ridzik's shoulders sagged. "Oh man, please tell me we aren't popping Cleanheads here. I hate the Cleanheads."

Gallagher grabbed Ridzik by the arm and pulled him aside. "Give us a second here, would you, Charlie?" Gallagher asked Stobbs.

"Yeah."

"Art," Gallagher hissed in Ridzik's face, "you're not helping yourself here. This is a good tip. This is hot and it's for real. Got it?"

Ridzik shook himself free. "You see me leaving?"

Gallagher jerked his head in Stobbs's direction. "He let you in on this," the detective

whispered. "He didn't have to. Now you're pissing him off." Gallagher lowered his voice even
more. "For Christ's sake, Art, this is the man
who's writing your fitness report. I thought
you wanted to come back. I really thought you
wanted it bad." Even as he was speaking, Tom
Gallagher wondered why he was bothering himself with the latest disaster to befall Art Ridzik's
career.

Ridzik wondered, too. If he didn't give a shit,
why the hell should Gallagher? He smiled. "No,
seriously Tom, I do want it. Look at me. I'm
pumped up. I got the edge. I'm drowning in
adrenaline."

"Please, Art. I need all the help I can get.
We've got a tough job and nobody loves us—
right?"

Ridzik nodded. Okay, he wouldn't pop Cleanheads for the sake of his own career, but he'd
give it a shot for the sake of Tom Gallagher's.
"Check," he said. "Let's do it."

Gallagher slapped Ridzik on the back. That
was more like it.

"Apartment 305," said Stobbs. Third floor.
The three men crept up the dark stairs, un-
holstering their weapons as they went. They
found the apartment, checked their weapons
one last time, knocked politely once, then Stobbs
threw his weight against the old wood, splin-
tering it.

The first thing the three cops saw when they
crashed into the tenement apartment was the
mound of crack on the bare wooden table in
the middle of the room, and the two black men

sitting there, carefully cutting the drug and packing it in smaller glassine envelopes.

The two men jumped to their feet, yelling and indignant.

"What the fuck is this man?"

"You got a warrant for this bullshit?"

The three detectives moved fast and sure, as if they had choreographed the raid beforehand. Ridzik and Gallagher slammed the two men against the cracked plaster wall and put their guns to the drug dealers' heads. The two men were both bald, their hair having been shaved down to the scalp—which was why they were called Cleanheads.

One of the Cleanheads looked over his shoulder at Ridzik, his dark brown eyes filled with hate and loathing for the detective.

"This is bullshit," he spat.

"Don't try anything smart, fuckhead." Ridzik stepped back from his man as Gallagher handcuffed both the dealers to stout heating pipes.

"Okay," said Stobbs. "You assholes are under arrest." He pulled a Miranda card from the pocket of his suit. "You have the right to remain silent."

Both Cleanheads remained silent.

"Anything you say can be used against you in court. You have the right to talk to a lawyer for advice before we ask you any questions and to have him with you during questioning."

Ridzik wandered around the room looking for any weapons or drugs that the cops could seize as evidence. On the far side of the room was a door, closed, maybe locked.

"If you cannot afford a lawyer, one will be appointed for you before questioning," Stobbs intoned. "If you decide to answer questions now without a lawyer present, you still have the right to stop questioning at any time."

Art Ridzik turned the doorknob, swung open the door, and gingerly stepped through. He sprung back into the room just as the deafening roar of a shotgun blasted away the doorframe.

"Holy shit!" yelled Gallagher.

The two Cleanheads did their best to hit the floor—no easy feat, considering their hands were cuffed to the pipes above their heads.

The three cops converged on the room. Ridzik heard the unmistakable sound of the shotgun being reloaded. He leapt into the doorway and fired, narrowly missing the third Cleanhead gunman who dashed through a side door into the corridor. Stobbs and Gallagher followed him. Ridzik didn't. He headed for the front door of the apartment.

"Art!" screamed Gallagher. "Where the fuck you—"

"Hey, man," shouted one of the cuffed Cleanheads. "What about us?"

Ridzik encountered the shotgunner on the stairs outside the apartment. He fired two big slugs at the man who dashed up the stairs toward the next floor. Gallagher and Stobbs arrived and started up the stairs after him. But Ridzik didn't. He ran down the stairs, away from the action.

"Sonovabitch!" yelled Stobbs. "As soon as we

get this motherfucker, I am personally going
to see that Ridzik—"

His words were drowned by the blast of the
shotgun from the gloom of the stairwell above
them. An old fire-hose box exploded, showering the two cops with glass chips.

"He's making me mad," said Stobbs through
gritted teeth. Gallagher didn't know if he was
talking about the Cleanhead or Ridzik.

"C'mon," urged Gallagher. The two cops
ducked out of their cover and climbed the stairs
four at a time.

The shotgunner made it onto the roof of the
building. Before going over the side to the fire
escape, which zigzagged down the side of the
tenement like an ugly stitch, he paused long
enough to blast away at Stobbs and Gallagher
at the door. Both cops dropped flat on the ooz-
ing tar paper.

The Cleanhead clambered down the metal
steps, watching over his shoulder for Stobbs
and Gallagher. He should have been looking
ahead of him, because the first indication he
got that Ridzik was anywhere in the neighborhood was when he felt the warm barrel of
Ridzik's gun pressed against his head.

"Freeze, motherfucker," hissed Ridzik.

The Cleanhead slowly turned his head and
saw a smiling Art Ridzik.

"Sheeit," said the Cleanhead.

"Now don't get nervous," said Ridzik. "I do
this for a living."

Gallagher and Stobbs came clambering down

the stairs. Gallagher laughed. "Art, you sonov-abitch. We thought you had lost your nerve."

"You might think something like that, Tom," said Ridzik innocently, "but Lieutenant Stobbs wouldn't think a thing like that. He knew what I was doing all along, didn't you, Lieutenant?"

Stobbs shook his head slowly and holstered his gun. "Read him his rights, Ridzik. And after these guys are booked I got another job for you two."

"Can't be as much fun as this," said Ridzik.

Art Ridzik and Tom Gallagher were in the international arrivals terminal at O'Hare International Airport promptly at 7:00 P.M. Customs was crowded as hundreds of people bustled through the big hall, toting their luggage toward the exit.

"I'll check to see if the flight is in here," said Gallagher, heading toward an information booth.

"Good thinking," mumbled Ridzik. "You do that." His eyes immediately locked on an attractive blond flight attendant. She was trundling her luggage along in front of her on one of those collapsible luggage carts. Ridzik had always had a yen to travel.

"Hi there. How you doin', honey?"

The blond's ice blue eyes swept over him. "Blow yourself."

"Thanks. Thank you very much. That's good thinking," he said evenly as she pushed past him, making for the door.

Gallagher returned. "The plane's in. He should be out any second."

"Uh-huh." Ridzik managed to tear his eyes away from the shapely ass of the attendant. "Hey, did you see Stobbs's report on the Clean-head action?"

"Yeah," said Gallagher. Ridzik wasn't going to like this. "He said your performance was 'adequate.'"

"Jesus Christ," said Ridzik, pulling a pack of cigarettes from his shirt pocket. "Adequate? That's all? Adequate?"

"Look, Art—"

"C'mon, Tom." Ridzik lit up. "If I had gone up the steps like you two guys that shithead would have gotten away." He exhaled heavily.

"Stobbs just didn't like you fooling with him like that. It made him look bad."

"Got the job done, didn't it?"

"Art," said Gallagher, *please*. It's a personality thing with him. Stobbs doesn't like yours."

"Personality? What about him? He's got the personality of a billboard."

"Look, I know you don't like him, but cool it. He just happens to be the guy filling out your fitness report, remember?"

Ridzik looked away, scanning the crowds. He drew on his cigarette again. "How can I forget."

"Take my advice. Humor him."

Art Ridzik dropped the half-smoked butt on the floor and ground it out with his heel. "All right, all right, big deal. Why the hell did we get stuck with this detail? And what is a Commie bastard doing in Chicago anyway?"

"The Commie bastard that our Commie bastard is taking home was a division collar,"

Gallagher explained patiently. "That's just one of the wonderful things that happened in the world of law enforcement when you were on suspension."

"Yeah, well, I'm sorry I missed it. It wasn't my idea to take twenty-one days enforced without pay, I might add. I'm sure that it was a high point in the history of East-West relations."

"I wouldn't say that, but it didn't hurt."

"Commies are devious, man. They want to take over the world, you know."

Gallagher sighed. This was a very simple assignment. Meet a Russian cop, drive him to his hotel; tomorrow morning, pick up the Russian cop, hand over the prisoner and say, "Have a nice flight." But Ridzik, as only Ridzik could, was bound to make it more complicated.

"Do me a favor, Art. Watch your mouth on this one. You could start World War III."

"That would not look good in my file."

Gallagher was scanning the crowds of people. "Now you're getting the idea ... How the hell are we supposed to recognize this guy?"

Ridzik, looking the other way, had an answer: "Tom, I have a feeling that is not going to be a problem."

Coming through the crowd was Captain Ivan Danko. Quite apart from his size, which was considerable, he would have stood out in any crowd. He was dressed in his full uniform of the Moscow Militia. It was a severe gray uniform, broken only by the red and gold epaulets on his broad shoulders and the red tabs on the collar. On his chest were two wide bars of decorations. He walked toward them, carrying his beat-up old suitcase.

"Look at those shoes," whispered Ridzik, staring at the thick rubber soles of Danko's shoes. "They look like he stole them off a tractor for Chrissake."

"Shuttup, Art."

"Bet he don't speak English, either."

Gallagher walked up to Danko. "Captain Danko?"

Danko stopped. "Yes?"

"I'm Detective Sergeant Gallagher, Chicago Police Department. Glad to meet you—welcome to Chicago."

No expression appeared on Danko's face. He didn't look happy or sad or even interested. Just impassive. "Thank you."

"This is my partner, Detective Sergeant Ridzik."

Ridzik waved.

"First time in Chicago?" asked Gallagher, which, he realized after he said it, was a pretty stupid question.

"Yes."

"Yeah," he said awkwardly. "Got any more luggage?"

"No."

"Any trouble with Customs?"

"Diplomatic immunity," said Danko.

Jeez, thought Ridzik. Eight syllables. Doesn't this guy ever shut up?

"Nice flight?" continued Gallagher gamely.

"Yes."

There was a moment of awkward silence.

"Hungry?"

"No," said Danko.

"Thirsty?"

"No."

"Look," said Ridzik, "can we gab someplace else? I'm parked in a red zone." He smiled at Danko. "No offense."

Danko sat in the backseat of Ridzik's beat-up sedan. The Russian cop ignored the beer cans, empty cigarette packs, and food wrappers littering the floor. He also seemed to do his best to ignore his hosts. Ridzik drove keeping an eye on his passenger in the rearview mirror. Gallagher, half turned in the front passenger seat, did his best to be friendly. Ridzik wondered why he bothered.

"Nice night," said Gallagher.

"Yes," said Danko.

"It's been real hot lately. Nothing is hotter than Chicago in August."

Danko didn't appear to be very interested in Chicago weather, but Gallagher battled on.

"It's the humidity that gets you."

Danko continued to stare out the window. Gallagher wondered if the Russian had understood what he was talking about.

"Humidity," said Ridzik, his eyes flicking up to the mirror. "You know. Moisture in the air."

Danko ignored him too. Ridzik shrugged. Just trying to be friendly.

"So, how's it been in Moscow?" asked Gallagher.

"Hot," he said. Danko's eyes met Ridzik's in the mirror. "No moisture."

Of course, thought Ridzik. Everything is wonderful in the worker's paradise. They've even abolished humidity. It's probably in a gulag somewhere.

"That's good," said Gallagher nervously. "Sounds nice." There was another awkward pause. Gallagher felt himself sweating under his lightweight jacket. This was hard work. He almost preferred busting Cleanheads to making conversation with this Russian stiff.

"If you were staying around longer, Captain, we could show you the sights. Chicago's got some great spots."

Heeey, thought Ridzik, that sounds like a barrel of laughs. Sure is a shame they wouldn't be able to get to know the captain a little better. He pressed down on the accelerator a little harder.

"It is very unfortunate," said Danko, as if he gave a damn. Viktor was the only thing on his mind. The sooner Danko left Chicago, the sooner he would return Viktor to Moscow and the justice he so richly deserved.

"Hey, Captain," said Ridzik, "where'd you learn English so good?"

"In Army," said Danko. "Compulsory training. Language school in Kiev."

Kiev, thought Ridzik. Now *that* sounded like a fun town. "Like chicken Kiev?"

Danko did not respond.

"So anyway, this Viktor Rosta musta really pissed off a few commissars or whatever for them to send someone all this way just to babysit him home. What did he do?"

Danko was ready with his answer, mindful of the major's orders to reveal nothing to the Americans. "Crimes against state."

"What did he do? Take a leak on the Kremlin wall?"

Gallagher shot Ridzik his "Art, for Chrissake" look. "I got to apologize for my partner here, Captain. He's naturally suspicious and—"

Ivan Danko showed his first burst of emotion. It wasn't much, but it was something. He interrupted Gallagher, cutting in hard. "Did _you_ arrest Viktor?" He leaned forward in his seat.

"Naw," said Gallagher. "A couple of the uniforms—you know, patrolmen. It was kind of an—"

"Where?"

"Right near this shitty hotel he lived in. The Garvin."

Ridzik scoffed. Some master criminal this Viktor Rosta must be. The Garvin! "No shit, he was staying at the Garvin? That hotel is a swamp. A breeding ground for pushers, pimps, hookers. Boy, the Garvin—"

Danko cut him off. "Take me there."

Ridzik and Gallagher exchanged worried looks. It would not look too good for them if the distinguished guest of the Chicago Police Department got robbed by a junkie in the Garvin Hotel.

"Look," said Gallagher, "we got you booked at the Executive House. It's a nice place, you'll like it."

"Please," Danko said, "the Garvin."

"He wants the Garvin, Tom," Ridzik said.

"I know, but—"

"I say we give the man what he wants."

Gallagher turned back to Danko. "Listen, if you're on a budget or something like that, I'm sure the department will spring for a little extra—"

"The Garvin," Danko said stolidly. He wanted to see the "swamp" that Viktor had lived in. No matter how bad it was, it would look like luxury compared to the place Danko would send him.

Gallagher sighed and shrugged. "Okay, the Garvin."

Ridzik drove through the hot streets of the South Side. Kids were out, playing in the fountains of water jetting from open hydrants. Entire families sat on the steps of their buildings, sipping beer and talking in the night, trying to beat the heat.

The Garvin had seen better days, but so long before, that no one remembered them. It was on a corner, facing the tracks of the elevated train that rumbled by the second-story window of the building every few minutes. The noise of the trains would wake the heaviest sleeper, but as far as Ridzik and Gallagher knew, very few people ever slept at the Garvin. It was a good place to score one of a dozen illegal pharmaceuticals or to spend some time with a hooker. But sleep there? It just wasn't done.

They pulled up to the front door of the hotel and all three cops got out of the car. Ridzik took Danko's bag out of the trunk while Gallagher made a last attempt to talk Danko out of his choice of hotel.

"It's not too late to change your mind. I'm telling you, this is a real pit."

"I will be fine, thank you."

"Okay," said Gallagher, bowing to the inevitable. "You're the boss. I'll pick you up at nine tomorrow."

"Nice talking to you, Captain," said Ridzik, sliding in behind the wheel. They watched as Danko walked into the hotel.

"What did you think of our buddy from Russia, Art?"

"I think he's a jerk," said Ridzik, pulling the car away from the curb.

The lobby of the Garvin Hotel gave a hint of the delights to be found in the bedrooms upstairs. There was a threadbare carpet on the floor, a piece of material so worn and dirty that you could only guess at what color it had been when new. There was a reception counter covered in a cracked and scratched sheet of plastic. Behind the desk sat a sallow, thin, unshaven young man who looked as if he had been hired specifically to fit into the Garvin's decorating scheme. In front of him on the desk was a baseball bat, although he didn't look like the sporting type. Tacked to the wall above his head was a hand-lettered sign:

PAY IN ADVANCE—SINGLE ROOM A NIGHT
DOUBLE BED—DOUBLE MONEY

The clerk looked up from a magazine as Danko entered. He wondered who the big dressed like a doorman was supposed to be and what he wanted from him.

"Danko," said Danko.

"You're welcome," said the clerk. He cackled a little hysterically at his own joke. Ivan Danko's face never changed expression.

"You want a room?" the night clerk asked.

"Yes."

The night clerk tossed a registration card at the Russian. "Just fill this out."

As Danko was writing his name in the strange Western alphabet, a cockroach scurried across the desk. The receptionist struck fast and hard with his baseball bat, cracking the desk again, but missing the roach. It darted to safety. Danko looked at him as if he were crazy.

"That's okay," said the clerk nervously. "All of the rooms are clean. Well, pretty clean."

"You had a man here called Rosta? Viktor Rosta?"

"A Russian?" asked the night clerk.

"I want same room."

"Hey, you a Russian, too? What, is there some kind of convention in town?"

Danko answered questions reluctantly, but he couldn't see that there was any harm in revealing his nationality, not if it would ensure him Viktor's old room. "I am Russian." He handed the clerk his form.

As he handed him his key, another cockroach appeared on the desk. Without hesitation, Danko smashed it to paste with his fist.

"Nice goin'," said the clerk. "Room 302."

Danko had not stayed in many hotels in his life, but he knew at once that room 302 was a dump. There was a sagging bed, a cigarette-scorched side table and a plastic-covered arm-chair. Oddly, though, the management had put a TV set in the room, a very good one—color, he discovered when he turned it on. Few hotels in the Soviet Union would have wasted a TV set on a room such as this one. As he stared at the screen, he was surprised to see a hazy, ugly pornographic film come on. Men and women were cavorting giggling and coupling in a bizarre variety of positions in a room which didn't look all that different from the one he was sitting in.

Danko didn't have too much trouble tearing his eyes away from the screen. Within an hour, he had meticulously taken room 302 apart. He had checked everywhere, including the inside of the toilet tank, for signs of Rosta's tenancy. But Rosta had left behind nothing, no sign that he had ever been there. And Danko was thorough. He had taken the mattress off the bed, ripped open the pillows, and stripped the pictures from the walls. He had pulled up the carpet. And he had discovered nothing but lint, dust, insects, and an old mousetrap. He looked unhappily at the ruins of the room. Before he left the next day, he would have to pay for the damage he had done. His few pre-cious dollars would have been well spent if he had found something. But, instead, he would be spending militia hard currency on nothing.

But he did have to pay. He could not vandalize a hotel room in a foreign country without making restitution. That would be a crime.

One item in the room puzzled him. On the table next to the bed was a square metal box which was connected to an electrical outlet in the wall. The box gave no indication as to its function. There was only a coin slot set in the top. Puzzled, Danko decided to risk a little more of his hard currency. He dropped a quarter into the slot. Suddenly, the bed began to buck and shake. Danko shook his head. He wondered if this was some device for waking yourself up in the morning. Then he glanced at the porn movie on the TV. No, he decided, this was some sort of booster for intercourse or masturbation.

He walked to the window and looked out. Across the street, at the level of his room window, was a giant billboard showing a lingerie-clad female with giant breasts. Her six-foot eyes leered into his. It was advertising for the neon-lit shop at street level. The sign said: "Adult Books. All Super X. Video-X. Marital Aids."

Danko looked at the shaking bed, the billboard, the porn store, and the movie on his television set.

"Kapitalism," he said disgustedly as an elevated train rocketed by his window.

Chapter Three

The next morning Ivan Danko stood in front of the Garvin Hotel in his full uniform, looking as if he belonged in that neighborhood about as much as a stripper would at a DAR convention. The Russian was still as talkative as he had been the night before and Tom Gallagher was still making a gallant effort to be friendly.

Danko refused Gallagher's offer of stopping for a cup of coffee, insisting that he be taken directly to the station house to sign the documents releasing Viktor to him. The precinct house was its usual riotous self. The old building was jammed with drunks and junkies and hookers who had been picked up the night before and were now on their way to court. The charge desk was jammed with dozens of people yelling at the booking sergeant in half a dozen languages—Spanish, Chinese, Polish—each person demanding that the cop on duty do something *now*. He grandly ignored all of them.

Danko looked disapprovingly at the chaos. This sort of thing would never be allowed to happen back home. Police stations were sacred, hushed fear-inspiring places. Ordinary citizens didn't go into them unless it was absolutely necessary.

Gallagher was glad that Danko showed some reaction, even if it was one of loathing and disgust. Anything was better than his great stone-face act.

"Looks like a major crime wave just hit, right?" he said, surveying the confusion. "I remember I thought the same thing the first time I came in here. But nope. It's just a typical Monday morning."

Danko nodded. More police, he thought. That was what America needed.

Gallagher looked across the room to a row of desks. At each sat a detective trying to interview criminals, argue with witnesses, answer the phone, and type, all at the same time. All of them were hard at it except for Art Ridzik. He sat at his desk, the scarred metal top covered in paperwork, playing chess on a small computerized chess set. He was studiously ignoring another detective who stood in front of him.

"Welcome back, Art," said Nelligan. "Listen, I want you to know there was nothing personal in what I did. I had to make a report and I made it. I didn't turn you in because you're you, I just—" The man shrugged. "Anyway, no hard feelings, right?" He stuck out his hand.

Ridzik looked up from his chess problem. "You say something, Nelligan?"

"Well, the hell with you, if that's the attitude you're gonna take."

"That's the attitude I'm going to take." Ridzik returned to his chess game. He was about to make a move when he heard Danko's voice.

"Not the king," growled the Russian.

Ridzik looked up, annoyed. "Why not?"

Danko scarcely glanced at the board, taking it all in quickly. His mind plotted a few moves further on assuming Ridzik would ignore his advice and move the king. "Checkmate in two moves."

"Really?" said Ridzik, unimpressed.

"Use bishop to queen four. Sicilian defense."

Ridzik sat back in his chair and looked at Danko. "Sicilian defense, huh? Listen, comrade, the last time I checked, Sicily was not part of the Soviet Union. I don't think I'll bishop to queen four if it's okay with you; I'm working on my own plan here." He returned to his game. "But thanks for all your help, comrade, I got it covered," he said dismissively.

"C'mon, Captain," said Gallagher. "Commander Donnelly is waiting to see you."

Without a word to Ridzik, Danko followed his guide. Ridzik moved the king. The computerized brain moved a rook. Ridzik moved his bishop for defense and the game beeped victoriously. His king had been checkmated by a red queen. It had taken two moves.

"Aw shit," muttered Art Ridzik. He tossed a glance in Danko's direction. "Do you fuckin' believe it?"

If you saw Commander Lou Donnelly on the

street, you would just assume he was a cop. He was tall and heavyset, a big man who looked like he had seen his fair share of law and disorder over the years. He also looked like the kind of guy who could handle himself on the streets. But he hadn't been a street cop for years. Now he was a senior officer, an administrator, an executive of the police department. Back when he had been struggling with street slime, he hadn't had a care in the world. He had never had a day's worth of sick leave. Now that all he had to do was deal with other cops—cops like Ridzik—he was a wreck.

His office did not look like a cop's office. It looked like a cross between a tropical fish shop and a botanical garden. On every flat surface a tank of brightly colored fish bubbled and the windows were festooned with leafy green plants. Danko didn't quite know what to make of it all.

Gallagher made introductions, and Danko and Donnelly had locked eyes for a second, each cop taking the measure of the other.

"This is the extradition order," Donnelly said, picking up a document from his desk. "All it requires is your signature."

Danko took the piece of paper in his big hands and studied it. "Has he asked for political asylum?"

Donnelly shook his head. "I think he's resigned to going home. He doesn't talk to us. We searched him, his car, his hotel room—he ran a red light, but didn't have a driver's license. Minor stuff, but he wouldn't speak English. Wouldn't say a thing, not even through an interpreter. He had a gun hidden in his car. That made things a little more serious. We saw his tattoo in Russian, we figured he was one of yours." Donnelly shrugged, as if to say "And here you are."

"The Moscow Militia is grateful to the Chicago Police," said Danko as if he were making a speech.

"Forget it. What do you guys want him for, anyway?"

Crimes against state, thought Gallagher.

The Moscow Militia was not so grateful to the Chicago Police that it felt it should tell them who they arrested and why he was wanted in the Soviet Union.

"Crimes against state," said Danko.

"That's not very specific," said Donnelly.

"He is a black marketeer."

"Neither is that."

"It's a crime."

"If you say so," said Donnelly. He picked up another document from his desk. "This is a quit claim. This states that we surrendered his personal effects to you." He read from the list: "Fifty-six dollars in cash, a key, and half a box of Crackerjack."

"Krakerjak?" It was the first English word he had encountered on this trip that mystified him.

"Candy," said Gallagher helpfully.

"Audrey," yelled Donnelly at his secretary, who sat at a desk just outside the office. "Go get Ridzik for me."

Both Gallagher and Danko had the same thought: Ridzik? What for?

"All of Viktor Rosta's stuff is at the city jail. You get that when you get him."

"Good," said Danko. His eyes had strayed to a tank of electric blue and yellow fish swimming around their little home without a care in the world.

"Stress management," explained Donnelly. "You get uptight, you're supposed to look at the fish, water the plants. Relax to pleasant sounds." He snapped on a tape recorder on his desk and soothing New Age music oozed into the room.

"Interesting," said Danko. He thought it was crazy. How could a small fish help a policeman?

"Personally, I think it's a load of bullshit, but when the alternative is major heart surgery you try anything."

Danko nodded.

"Out of curiosity, Captain, since I figure cops are cops if they're here or in the Soviet Union or Switzerland, for that matter—how do you guys in Moscow deal with tension and stress?"

"Vodka," said Danko. It was the closest Gallagher had heard him come to a joke.

"Vodka," said Donnelly. "Maybe I'll try that next."

Ridzik pushed into the room. He had attempted to be the cop Gallagher wanted him to be. He had straightened his tie and put on his jacket.

"Yes, sir, what can I do for you, sir?"

Donnelly shot a look at Ridzik. He wasn't

sure he liked Ridzik to be so accommodating. "Ride with the captain here over to the city jail. See that he signs the forms when he gets the prisoner and bring the top copy back to me."

Ridzik frowned. This wasn't being a cop, it was being an office boy, a messenger.

Donnelly turned his attention back to Danko. Solemnly they shook hands. "So long, Captain," he said. "Nice doing business with you."

After the two Chicago cops had left with the Russian in tow, Commander Donnelly watered his plants and fed his fish and reflected that Viktor Rosta was one problem at least that would not affect the delicate state of his cardiovascular system. It wasn't a bad idea: arrest 'em all and pack them off to Russia. He returned to his duty rosters. That, he thought, was that.

He was wrong.

Viktor Rosta was not particularly surprised to see Ivan Danko, but that didn't make him hate him any less. Danko had killed his brother. Danko would have to pay. The big Russian policeman had snapped a handcuff on one of Rosta's wrists and had looped the metal band around his own, snapping it shut and locking it. He looked at Rosta impassively, his face not betraying the loathing he felt for the criminal; neither did he show the elation he felt at finally having him in custody.

"I'm taking you home to die, Viktor," he said.

Rosta sneered. "Eat shit, Danko."

For once, Danko's anger overcame his iron self-control. He slammed the Russian up against the dull gray cinder-block wall of the cell and hissed in his ear: "Or would you rather die here? It makes no difference to me."

Ridzik turned to Gallagher. "Look, you can tell they're old friends. Body language is a beautiful thing."

"Ahh, Captain . . ." said Gallagher. He wanted the two Russians to get out of Chicago, preferably alive. A dead prisoner in a holding cell would be very bad news.

Danko managed to calm himself down. He released Rosta and smoothed down his uniform. "We're ready to go."

"Good."

The next stop was the property room. A clerk delivered the manila envelope containing the belongings taken from Rosta when he was arrested. Danko examined each one carefully. The money was of no interest, but he dumped out the Crackerjack box, even opening the little envelope that contained a plastic whistle. He held up the key.

"What does this open, Viktor?"

"Kiss my ass."

Danko dangled the key in front of Ridzik. "Anyone know who opens this?"

Ridzik glanced at the key with little interest. "Looks like the key to some kind of locker. Why don't you get your friend to tell you?" He nodded at Viktor. "You know, what with you being able to speak the language."

"I have tried."

"I'll try in English." Ridzik leaned forward till he was in Rosta's face. "Where-is-the-locker-that-this-key-opens, comrade?" he said slowly, as if speaking to a child.

Viktor stared him in the face and said nothing.

Ridzik could see how this kind of behavior could piss a guy off. "Hey, listen you Soviet pile of shit, I just asked you a question."

Viktor smiled and spoke in Russian.

"What did he say?"

Danko translated carefully. "He asked why you don't go and fuck your mother's ass."

"Huh," said Ridzik. "I'm really impressed, Captain. They teach you the dirty words and everything at that school in Kiev." Ridzik nodded. "Very good." Then, faster than anyone expected, Ridzik flew across the table, his hands closing on Viktor's neck. He snapped the Russian's head against the wall. "You little sonova-bitch," he said through gritted teeth.

"Jesus, Art!" yelled Gallagher. It took the combined strength of Danko and Gallagher to pull Ridzik off Rosta. Gallagher wished that Ridzik would stop making his life so damn difficult. First the Russian tries to kill the Russian. Now Ridzik tries it. Gallagher was going to be very glad to see that plane take off.

"Art, that's enough, for chrissakes."

"He shouldn't have said that about my mother," grumbled Ridzik.

"Look, if we're going to make that plane we are going to have to get a move on."

"We go," said Danko.

They made their way toward the exit. Ridzik folded the documents he had to return to his commander and put them in his inside pocket. Rosta and Danko trailed behind.

"I don't care if the guy *is* a fuckin' criminal," said Ridzik, "he still shouldn't say anything about someone's mother."

Gallagher rolled his eyes. "What the hell do you care what he says? What do you care what he says about anything? It's not your case, Art. It's not my case." Gallagher glanced over his shoulder at Danko. "For Chrissake, it's not even an *American* case."

"Right," said Ridzik. "Drop it, would ya?"

But Gallagher wouldn't drop it. "We're an escort service here. Jesus, pull back your emotions."

"C'mon, Tom, you heard what the shithead said. I couldn't let that pass."

"You're gonna have to find some middle ground, learn to roll with the punches."

"Yeah, yeah." He glanced toward the door. Four security guards, three black guys and one white guy—rent-a-cops—were coming into the building. For a moment, Ridzik thought this was strange. Then he remembered that the Parking Violations Bureau on the fifth floor took in a lot of cash in traffic fines. This must have been a routine money pickup. They were all wearing sunglasses.

"Well, Captain," said Ridzik. "This is it. I say good-bye here. Have a great flight." He glanced at Viktor. "And hey, Danko, if you get a chance to flush this giant turd down the toilet, do it over the Pole. Tom, I'll catch you back at the office."

"Sure thing, Art."

Ridzik strolled across the lobby of the building and bought himself a newspaper and a racing tip sheet. He figured he would head for a diner, get something to eat, and check out the ponies before going back to work. First day back on the job he didn't want to overdo things.

"Gimme a *Sun Times* and a *Racing Action* tipsheet." The newsie folded the sheet into the paper and handed them to Ridzik.

"You got a winner? You wanna share the wealth?"

Ridzik laughed wearily. "You kiddin'. They've been beating my ass off lately. I feel like the Cubs."

The four guards that Ridzik had noticed split into two pairs, two guys on either side of Rosta, Danko, and Gallagher. Of the three men, only Rosta noticed them. As they drew abreast of the guards, one of the black guys whipped out a cut-down baseball bat and smashed Danko hard on the back of the head. He dropped to the floor, the pain in his head the only thing keeping him semiconscious. He gave his body orders, but it didn't respond. Through the haze of pain, he knew what was happening: Rosta was being rescued. As if from far away, he heard a gun go off twice.

Both slugs, fired by the white guy, slammed into Gallagher. The first one hit him in the

chest, wounding him seriously. The second tore
into his heart. It killed him.

Rosta stretched the handcuff chain between
him and Danko tight. One of the black guys
produced a set of heavy wire cutters and
snapped the links with ease. As soon as his
hands were free, Rosta reared back and smashed
Danko furiously in the mouth.

"What you doin', man?" screamed one of the
Cleanheads. "Let's get the fuck out of—"

Rosta was rummaging through Danko's pockets as if he was rolling a drunk in an alleyway.

"Let's go! Let's go!"

"The key," mumbled Rosta.

The white guy was waving his gun around
the room. Everyone in the lobby had dived for
cover when the first shot had been fired. Except for Ridzik.

He crouched in the combat stance, took careful aim, and blew the white guy away, whose
gun clattered across the floor.

"Fuck this," said one of the Cleanheads and
grabbed Rosta by the collar, yanking him to
his feet. As he lurched, the key Viktor had had
in his hand went flying.

"Haul ass!" yelled someone.

They went flying out the door and tumbled
down the steps of the jail, making for a station
wagon that stood in the street, its engine fired
up. Ridzik paused just long enough at the body
of his friend to make sure there was nothing
he could do for him. Gallagher was dead, and
someone was going to pay. Ridzik took off.

As he came out of the building, he was greeted

with the blast of a shotgun fired from the station wagon. He ducked, brought his gun up
and found himself staring into the horrified
eyes of a woman who had been headed into the
building. A split second later he would have
shot her, but he managed to hold his fire.

"Sonovabitch! Get out of the way!" But the
woman was immobilized by fear. Ridzik ran
around her and hit the street. Cars screeched
to a halt. Horns blared. He fired three shots at
the station wagon, which was burning rubber,
fishtailing up the street and gone.

Ridzik exhaled heavily and let the gun drop
to his side. They had got away and Tom
Gallagher was dead. Killed for being too much
of a nice guy. This war was just beginning.

Inside the building all was pandemonium.
People were screaming. The guy Ridzik had
dropped groaned in pain and shock. Gallagher
was ominously still. Danko managed to raise
his head. Through his pain-clogged eyes he
could just make out, lying on the blood-slick
floor, the key. Viktor Rosta's key. With super-
human effort he managed to crawl the few feet
to the key and he grasped it tightly in his
hands.

Chapter Four

The pain Danko felt, as he lay in his hospital bed, had nothing to do with his injuries—it was much more severe than a crack on the mouth and a blow on the head. The pain he felt was the pain of having failed: not having failed his masters in the militia, but in having failed himself and the memory of his partner, Yuri. He had sworn that he would get Rosta, and he would, but it would not be as easy as he had once thought it would be. He still held the key in his hand.

A pretty, young black woman, an intern, was looking into his eyes with a small flashlight. She nodded to herself, made a note on his chart, and consulted some X rays on a light box next to the bed.

"That was some crack on the head you took yesterday. How you feeling?"

Danko stared at her. He was feeling like a failure and a fool. He said nothing.

"That good?" She picked up his wrist and glanced at her watch as she took his pulse.

"The blow has left you with a slight concussion. To be on the safe side we'll be keeping you here a couple of days."

Danko didn't think they would be keeping him here. Not while Viktor Rosta was out there, free. His uniform was nowhere to be seen, but he noticed that his suitcase was on the chair on the far side of the room. He didn't need his uniform. He was going undercover.

Ridzik and Lieutenant Stobbs waited outside the operating theater, one floor down from Ivan Danko's room. They leaned against the wall, ignoring the bustle in the busy hospital corridor. The white guy Ridzik had shot was having his second bout of surgery. He would be able to give them some valuable information—if he lived—and that would help immeasurably. Right now, half the Chicago police force was running around like chickens with their heads cut off, trying to find Gallagher's killers.

Nothing galvanizes a police force quite like the killing of one of their own. It didn't matter that the mayor would go to Gallagher's funeral or that thousands of Chicagoans would donate money to a trust fund for Gallagher's widow. The only result the cops wanted was his killer's skin. When a cop died, things got hot on the street. The police called in their favors and leaned heavily on the drug, gambling, fencing and hooking operations until the street people turned into snitches. Killing a cop was bad for business—usually. But this time, even with the heat on high, no one had said a thing.

"I can't believe it," said Ridzik. "They have

disappeared into thin air. The car, the Commie, the entire ambush team."

"Except this one," said Stobbs with something approaching admiration. He jerked his thumb toward the operating room.

"How is the shithead?"

"Good as you get with a hole in your chest. When are you going to grace us with one of your colorful reports, Art?"

Ridzik worked hard to control his anger. His partner had been blown away and Stobbs wanted a report. "Soon as I get to a typewriter, Lieutenant."

"How about giving me a preview?"

Ridzik shrugged. He had been over it a dozen times already. "The whole thing went ballistic. You aren't really thinking about reports though, when someone is seriously considering ways of killing you." He shifted the weight from one leg to the other as if nervous, impatient to get out in the street and kick some ass. "Tell you one thing, though, I think that the black dudes were the same Cleanheads we busted the day before yesterday. I know it sounds crazy. I mean, if we can give anyone a clean it's those guys, right?"

Stobbs shook his head. "They walked."

"They _what?_"

"They walked yesterday morning. Illegal warrant."

"Hold it, hold it, hold it. What about the one with the shotgun? I might be wrong on this but I seem to recall shooting at people with a shotgun is illegal, warrant or no warrant."

Stobbs shook his head sadly. This was something even he and Ridzik could agree on. "With an illegal warrant we wouldn't—shouldn't—have been there. If we weren't there, that asshole couldn't shoot at us with a shotgun."

"But what if he had killed someone? You telling me he would have walked if he had greased you or me or—"

"Argue with the judge, Art, not me."

"Sonovabitch."

"You want to hear something strange?"

"Stranger that what you just told me?" said Ridzik acidly.

"This one, the one you dropped—"

"Yeah?"

"Guess where he's from."

"Are you shittin' me? Not another one."

"That's right. Russia. Can you believe that? Another one. The whole city must be full of them."

"Well, two more flew in today, least that's what Donnelly told me."

Stobbs's eyes narrowed suspiciously. "Who? Which two? Bad guys?"

"Depends on how you look at it," said Ridzik.

They were diplomats, flown in from the Russian Embassy in Washington. They were the first people to be allowed to question Danko. The senior of the two, Gregor Moussorsky, did the talking. He was a slim, Westernized Soviet, smooth and wise to the ways of handling Americans. His superior, Dmitri Stepanovitch, was more like the type of Soviet bureaucrat

Danko was used to dealing with: dour, stone-faced, dressed in a baggy gray suit.

"We need to know what happened," said Moussorsky in Russian. "The Comrade Consul must make a full report to Moscow."

Danko knew exactly what was going on. Moussorsky and Stepanovitch would make their report, blame Danko, and everyone would be satisfied. It would be the end of Danko's career, he might even spend some time in jail, a scapegoat punished. But the two diplomats didn't understand. Danko wasn't working for them anymore. He was now his own boss.

"There is nothing to report."

"Your attitude is disappointing." Moussorsky meant it. He had read and memorized Danko's file. He was an excellent police officer, decorated many times for bravery, considered loyal by his superiors. He could have gone far. Not after this disaster, of course, but he didn't have to make things harder for himself *and* them.

"He got away. You can get the details from the Americans."

"The Americans are already asking too many questions. There is no reason for us to wash our dirty linen in public."

It struck Danko that that was exactly what Major Bondarev had said. Danko did not reply. The two diplomats exchanged looks, exasperated. Stepanovitch, a security attaché at the embassy—or so his passport said—was actually one of the KGB staffers in the Russian compound. He wished he could apply some of the less subtle methods his branch of the service employed.

"Viktor Rosta escaped," he said in his cold, flat voice. "He escaped because of your stupidity. He is free to complete his deal and send the American poison home through his network. You have failed completely."

But I won't fail again, thought Ivan Danko.

"That is my report."

"Report it however you please." Danko also noticed that Stepanovitch was only concerned about Viktor. Much as he wanted to find the gangster and kill him in revenge for the death of Yuri, Danko had not forgotten Gallagher. He was a cop and he was dead. Danko would not forget him either.

Stepanovitch smiled thinly. "I already have. Militia Headquarters has instructed me to tell you that when you are discharged from this hospital you will be taken to the airport and sent back to Moscow. You will report immediately for disciplinary hearings."

If Stepanovitch thought he was frightening Danko he was mistaken. "Tell Moscow that I am staying until Viktor Rosta is captured." Or dead, he added silently.

Ridzik and Stobbs were waiting for the two Soviet diplomats when they emerged from Danko's room.

"How is he?" asked Stobbs.

"He is very grateful for medical attention and very anxious to return to the Soviet Union," he said smoothly like a good diplomat.

Grateful? thought Ridzik. Anxious? That didn't sound like his old pal Ivan Danko.

"Who are you, please?" asked Stepanovitch.

"My name's Stobbs. Lieutenant Stobbs, Chicago Police Department. I'm the field officer in charge of this investigation. Can I have a word with you?"

The two Soviet diplomats didn't want to have a word with anyone, least of all a member of the Chicago police force. Danko was causing trouble, Rosta was at large, an American policeman was dead—none of this made their country look good. More important, it didn't reflect well on Moussorsky and Stepanovitch. They liked living in the West and didn't want a recalcitrant militiaman and a filthy drug dealer to destroy their carefully tended careers. But there was no escaping Stobbs or the general anger of the Chicago police. Even cold, dour Stepanovitch recognized that.

"We will be glad to assist in any way possible," he said.

"Good. I was hoping you could tell us what Viktor Rosta was doing here in the first place. Your Captain Danko was pretty tight-lipped on the subject."

Well, thought Stepanovitch, at least Danko followed one order.

"Rosta is wanted for crimes in the Soviet Union," said Moussorsky.

Stobbs rolled his eyes. "Yeah, we figured that. The thing that really interests us is his connection to the Cleanheads."

"Cleanheads?" said Moussorsky blankly.

"A very tough gang. Very mean and into a

lot of very nasty business. Drugs, extortion, murder for hire . . ."

Moussorsky's brows knit. "And they are connected with Rosta?"

"We figured they are the ones who sprung him."

"Very mysterious." He consulted quickly with Stepanovitch in Russian. His superior's instructions were succinct: tell him nothing.

"Yes, very mysterious. We have no information on the subject." He paused as if searching his mind for a logical answer. "Perhaps they are friends?"

"Oh, for Chrissake," breathed Ridzik, who was loitering a few feet away, listening to the conversation. "This is the old red runaround." Stobbs shot him a very angry look.

"Get lost, Ridzik."

Art Ridzik thought that wasn't a bad idea. He ambled down the corridor, turned a corner, and walked straight into Danko's room. The captain had gotten out of bed and dressed in civilian clothes. He would win no prizes for his taste in clothes and would make the best-dressed list only in Vladivostok, if it had one. The suit was pure polyester—Ridzik figured that if it caught fire he would die of the fumes—and looked as if it had been tailored by the same guy who designed the Chernobyl nuclear plant.

But Ridzik wasn't that interested in Danko's clothes. What caught his eye was Danko's taste in accessories. Ivan Danko was clutching a heavy piece of weaponry. It looked to Art to be 7.63 mm at least.

"How the hell did you get that through Customs?"

"In suitcase," said Danko. He holstered the gun in a shoulder brace.

"Guess that's an advantage of diplomatic immunity. How come you aren't wearing your nice uniform?"

"Now I work undercover."

Undercover? In *that* suit? thought Art. Anyway, forget the clothes; Danko would still tend to stand out on Chicago's mean streets. If anyone looked like a Russian, and a Russian cop at that, it was Captain Ivan Danko.

"Oh, you're gonna fit right in," scoffed Ridzik. "Detective Ivan Gumby. Get serious."

Danko snapped shut his suitcase. He had no time to listen to Ridzik. It was Rosta he was after.

"Okay," said Ridzik, "forget it, some people got fashion sense, others don't. I want you to tell me what Rosta is up to."

"I go."

"No," said Ridzik. "You stay. Lemme guess. Drug deal right? Drugs were the Cleanheads' most lucrative operation. They'll get anything you want and in any quantity. I figure your pal Rosta is buying wholesale, right? You tell me the nuts and bolts of the deal, and you get to keep your gun. Your secret is safe with me."

The muscles in Danko's jaw tensed. "You want the gun, you'll have to take it."

"Aw c'mon, give it a rest, comrade," said Ridzik wearily. "Maybe that kind of bully-shit works on the chessboard, but I've seen your moves on the street, bubba. Pathetic. Really pathetic."

Danko felt himself getting hot with shame and embarrassment. Ridzik had a point. Danko had walked straight into a trap, never saw the ambush coming.

"And while you were rolling around on the ground picking concrete out of your teeth, I bagged one of them. He's in Intensive Care right now. And he's another Russian. You should drop in and talk to him."

"Russian? What is his name."

"Tell me about Rosta."

Danko shook his head. He picked up his suitcase. "I'll go find him." He opened the door and walked out into the corridor, Ridzik at his heels. Stobbs, still hanging around in the corridor, was surprised to see the two of them.

"What the hell you doing out of bed, Danko?"

Danko strode purposefully down the corridor.

"Answer me, dammit," barked Stobbs.

"He said he's going to find Viktor," said Ridzik.

Stobbs planted himself squarely in front of the big Russian, stopping him in his tracks.

"Danko, we already got five hundred guys looking for his ass."

"Maybe I help," said Danko.

"Yeah," said Ridzik, "maybe he help."

"Shuttup. Danko, the last time you helped, one of our guys got blown away."

"I did not anticipate American criminals would help Viktor."

"Shit on that, Danko. Like it was *our* fault. We got enough trouble in this town without

having to import our hard guys from Russia."
Stobbs jabbed a finger into Danko's rock-hard
chest. "And let me tell you something else,
Captain. He isn't your prisoner anymore."

"Glasnost him, Lieutenant," said Ridzik.

"Shuttup. Rosta killed a cop. When we arrest him, we won't be sending his ass back to
Moscow."

Danko said nothing, but he thought: I'll have
to kill him here, then.

"Ridzik!"

"What?"

"Look, keep an eye on this guy. He's a material witness now. I gotta talk to Donnelly—
maybe he can figure out what to do with this
guy."

"I don't need Ridzik."

"The hell with what you need, Danko. You
do what you're told." Stobbs turned to Ridzik.
"Art, you watch this guy. He fucks up, it's your
ass."

"That's a hard invitation to turn down."

"Just do it." Stobbs headed for the elevator.

Danko stood stock-still in the middle of the
hospital corridor, watching Stobbs walk away.
"He blames me for Sergeant Gallagher's death."

"He might have a point there, comrade."

Danko shook his head slowly. "In Moscow
we do not pass the book."

"The buck," corrected Ridzik.

"What is *buck?*"

"Never mind."

Much as Danko hated to admit it, he did
need Ridzik. He needed just a little informa-

tion to get started. Once he was launched, he figured he could take it from there.

"The Negro men that helped Viktor—"

"Cleanheads. Probably Elijah Brothers—a jailhouse gang. You got prison gangs in Russia?"

"Yes. But they stay in prison."

"Novel solution," said Ridzik. "Here they get out and move right back on the streets. These guys are real big into the drug business, which brings me back to the guess I made in your room. Viktor? Remember?"

"Viktor in drug business too."

Ridzik was surprised. Danko had finally said something, something of importance. "Now we're getting somewhere."

Danko nodded. "You help?"

"Help nothin', Danko. I *am* this investigation. Tom Gallagher was a friend of mine."

"And Viktor is my enemy."

"So we got something in common. That doesn't make us partners."

Danko was tired of arguing. "Please, drive me to Hotel Garvin. Then we find Viktor."

Ridzik gave Danko a long look. Much as he hated to admit it, Danko held pieces of the puzzle in his head that Art Ridzik needed. He decided he'd play along with the Russian just long enough to learn what he needed, then it was "Sayonara, comrade." Or whatever.

"Let's go."

The hotel clerk was surprised to see Danko back again. He looked up from his magazine. "Nice suit," he said.

The clerk wasn't the only one surprised to

see Danko back at the Garvin. Parked across
the street from the hotel, slung low in his seat
was a member of Viktor's gang, a Russian
named Joseph Baroda. He saw Danko enter
the building and swore under his breath. It
had been a mistake not to kill the militiaman
when they had the chance.

The hotel clerk shook his head slowly. "I
can't give you your old room, man. There's a
lady just checked in. She wouldn't take any
other room in the place. What is it about that
room anyway?"

"The view," said Danko. "Give me the room
next door."

"All yours, bud."

Danko placed his suitcase in his room and
then stepped out into the hall and listened at
the door of his old room. He had torn the place
apart looking for some trace of Viktor Rosta
and had found nothing. Now a woman demands
the same room. It was too much to be simple
coincidence. There was something in that room
and Danko wanted it. He listened hard in-
tently. He could hear a shower pounding within
and beneath that sound a faint scratching of
wood and metal. He tried the door handle.
Locked.

Inside the room, Cat Menzetti, a dark, lithe
beautiful young woman, knelt on the floor of
the room. She had pulled back the worn carpet
and was carefully unscrewing a length of floor-
board. The screws came easily out of the old
wood. In a matter of minutes she had removed a
length of flooring. She thrust her hand into the

dark hole and pulled out a plastic bag. In it she could see a passport and one-half of a hundred-dollar bill. She shook her head. What the hell was this all about?

Working quickly, she started to screw the plank back into place. She had three screws—one to go—back in the floor when she heard the doorknob turning and the lock cracking. She blanched, throwing the carpet back over the bare board and spitting the last screw in her mouth onto the floor. Someone was simply breaking through the lock and there was nothing she could do to stop whoever the hell it was coming in. Time to swing into plan B.

She kicked off her shoes and started to pull up her tight cotton T-shirt. Her head was swathed in material, her full breasts exposed, when the door opened. Through the gauzy material she could tell that whoever it was in the doorway was no one she knew. Time to become a hooker, she thought, setting up for a night's business. She pulled the T-shirt over her head. She looked the big guy straight in the eye, holding the shirt across her breast.

"I was just going to take a shower," said Cat Manzetti, her voice dead calm—pretty good acting, she thought. "You wanna join me, it'll cost you fifty bucks. And by the way, I don't like it when people point guns at me."

Danko lowered the gun he had aimed at her bare chest. "I want to talk to you," he said.

Holy shit, she thought, another Russian. "Yeah, they all say that, hon."

"I have no interest in your body," he said.

"Oh, a charmer." She shrugged. "The price is the same if we talk or take a shower." She picked up her small bag. Stowed within it was the little plastic bag containing the things she had taken out of the floor. She started toward the bathroom. "Last chance," she said over her shoulder.

"I will wait." Danko sat on the edge of the bed. The bathroom door closed. The shower continued to pound.

Abruptly he stood and walked to the window. Ridzik was standing, leaning against the fender of his car. He was glancing impatiently at his watch. Danko had noticed Ridzik's watch. It was nice.

He turned back to the bathroom door. For some reason, he glanced at his feet. There, lying on the rug was a screw. He knelt and picked it up. He pulled back the carpet and saw the hole that the screw was supposed to fill. He wanted to shout with anger. He had been stupid, again. He had torn the room apart, but had failed to look at the floorboards. He slapped his fist into his hand. And he had made another mistake. He had assumed the woman was a prostitute as she had pretended. She had whatever had been hidden here.

He threw his full weight against the bathroom door, twisting the flimsy door off its hinges. The dingy bathroom was filled with steam, the water from the shower rained down, and a door leading out into the hallway stood open a bit. The woman, whoever she was, had gone.

Chapter Five

Danko sat at Ridzik's desk, poring over the chess problem that Ridzik had left set up on the board. He moved his knight, and the computerized brain countered with a rook. Danko nodded, swept his bishop diagonally across the board, and checkmated the machine. The computer squealed electronic annoyance. The easy victory did not please Danko. He recalled Ridzik's words: he might be tough on a chessboard, but out in the street, these American streets, he couldn't do anything right. First Viktor, now the girl . . .

Ridzik was in Donnelly's office. The commander stared out through a green curtain of plants, watching Danko. This was getting ridiculous. Donnelly had enough trouble with his own guys.

"Look," Ridzik was saying. "All I did was drive him back to his hotel. He checked in. Ten minutes later he was back outside and told me about some broad taking a shower. I didn't know what the hell else to do, so I brought him back here."

Donnelly shook his head. "Okay, okay. I guess he's our baby right now. But you know what we have to do, right?"

"What, with him?"

"No, Art, with you."

"Me?"

"You know how it is. If a police officer is a witness to a murder, then you do not actively participate in the investigations."

"Son of a—"

Donnelly cut through the interruption. "I know, I know. I'm not taking you off the case. You and Gallagher were friends, so I'll fit you in somewhere. Just remember that officially it's not your case. Now send in the Russian and get Stobbs."

Before Danko entered the office, he pulled Ridzik aside. "I have been thinking."

"Great, now you want to defect, right?"

"The escape of Viktor. It was arranged while he was in jail."

"Brilliant."

"Find out who visited him while he was in jail."

Ridzik hated to admit it, but that was not a bad idea. He told himself he would have thought of it himself, in time. He picked up a phone, dialed a number. "Gloria? Art Ridzik. Listen, you think you could do me a favor?" Gloria, one of the departmental secretaries, was used to doing Ridzik favors. "Can you find out who visited the Russian in jail? R-o-s-t-a, Viktor

with a *k*. Love you." He turned back to Danko.
"Okay, time to see Donnelly."

Stobbs had been busy. "This is what we got
so far. The two diplomats have gotten a little
friendlier. They called someone in and came
back all smiles and help. They are sort of pin-
ing to see you again, Captain."

Danko nodded. He would surrender to them
when the job was done.

"They also gave me some information." Stobbs
read from a sheet on a clipboard. "Viktor Rosta
was born in 1949 in Georgia—the Russian Georgia, not ours. Crime seems to run in the family. His father had the distinction of being tried
by the Germans and shot by the Russians for a
crime called *brigandage*." The three American
cops looked at Danko. "What's *brigandage?*"
asked Stobbs.

"Burn villages, rape women."

"That kind of thing goes on in Russia?" asked
Ridzik.

"In past, during great patriotic war. Not now."

"Anyway," continued Stobbs, "Viktor spends
three years in the army and six in a labor
camp for drug offenses. He is wanted in the
Soviet Union for murder, rape, extortion, kid-
napping, currency dealing, and drug dealing."

Danko nodded, that was about right.

"This is not a nice guy," observed Donnelly
professionally.

Danko was amazed at the quality of the information the Chicago cops had gotten their
hands on. He couldn't quite believe that the
Soviet Embassy in Washington had authorized

this. "Where did you receive this information from?"

"Told you," said Stobbs. "Your guys."

"Yeah," said Ridzik, "they'll probably send over some caviar later."

"Can you fill in some blank spots for us, Captain?" said Donnelly. "It's nice to know who Viktor's dad was, and the details of Viktor's record, but maybe you might be able to tell us what he's up to now. Specifically, what the hell is he doing in Chicago?"

Danko looked from Stobbs to Ridzik and then back at Donnelly. If he was going to find Viktor, he was going to have to take these men into his confidence.

"Viktor is shipping cocaine from America into Soviet Union. He has done it twice before—each time bigger shipment. He has accomplices here, Soviet citizens. Georgians."

Donnelly folded his arms across his chest. "Why didn't you tell us this before?"

"No authorization."

"Bullshit," said Stobbs.

"If we had known that Viktor was into some heavy shit with the Cleanheads, we would have been better set up to make sure they didn't pull anything," said Ridzik bitterly. Unspoken was the statement that all of them could hear in their heads: and Tom Gallagher would still be alive.

Donnelly held up his hands as if quieting Ridzik down. "Is there anything else my men need to know, Captain?"

Danko nodded. "You must know that I will

not leave your country without Viktor. I need cooperation."

Stobbs and Donnelly exchanged looks. Donnelly nodded. "You want to stick around," said the commander casually, as if Danko were going to be an interested observer. "Well, I got no problem with that. Fine by me."

"I need one man. Show me around city."

"Fine," said Donnelly. "You can have Ridzik."

"Oh jeez," said Ridzik. "Sir—"

"Told you I'd fit you in, Art. It's the best I can do. Take it or leave it."

"I'll take it," said Ridzik. He knew when he was beat and he couldn't really fault Donnelly. He was a fair man and he knew that he had to go strictly by the book on this one if they were going to send Viktor away for a long, long time. If he made a procedural mistake, the defense would be all over them.

"That okay with you, Captain?" asked Donnelly.

Danko nodded shortly. Now there's a big, warm vote of support, thought Ridzik. A breakthrough in superpower relations.

"Good," continued Donnelly. "Now I have a couple of recommendations for the both of you. It's gotta be low profile. I don't want the press near you. Got it?"

"Order them to stay away," said Danko.

"Well, you see Captain, it doesn't quite work like that over here."

"But you are the police," said Danko as if that explained everything.

"Yeah, that's true but the media don't see it that way. So, I don't want you rolling through town like the Red Army. We're gonna find Rosta." Donnelly leaned forward and rested his arms on the desk. *"We're* gonna nail his ass to the wall. Take my word for it."

Danko would like to have believed that, but he didn't. He wasn't completely ignorant of the American criminal justice system. "Your courts let the criminals go if they say they are sorry. I do not want this for Viktor."

Donnelly had to suppress a smile. Every cop thought that the courts were too lenient with hardened repeat offenders, but not one that he knew of thought they were that easy on them. Besides, there wasn't a cop on the force in Chicago or anywhere else—he hoped—who would have exchanged the American system for the Soviet. Still, he could see Danko's point. Viktor wouldn't beat the rap, but with the right lawyer he might get less than the prison stretch he deserved.

"We'll make sure that Rosta does time. A lot of it—like the rest of his life," Donnelly spoke with a confidence he didn't really feel. "But in the meantime, I don't want you messing this up, got it?"

"I will not make another mistake."

"Just so long as you realize you have been making mistakes," said Stobbs.

"Yeah, up to now it seems like we're the guys who've been catching Rosta," said Ridzik, "and it's you guys who have been letting him get away. Am I right?"

"It will not happen again." Watching Danko leave the office with Ridzik, Stobbs had a feeling that the big Russian just might be right.

"A pretty determined guy," he observed. "But let me ask you something, Commander." He paused as if searching for exactly the right words. "Have you, by any chance, completely lost your mind?"

Donnelly was staring at one of his fish tanks. "What makes you say that?" He snapped on some of his soothing New Age music. It made Muzak sound like Bon Jovi.

"Danko and Ridzik? That's the best combination of weirdos since Bonnie and Clyde."

Donnelly smiled. "Danko's the perfect weapon, Charlie. A loose cannon. If he helps us get Rosta—great. And if he breaks rules, screws up along the way"—Donnelly shrugged—"he's a Russian. Not our problem. Let some commissar in Moscow do something about it. Not our problem."

"Yeah, but what happens if he screws up to the tune of shooting some innocent Chicagoan bystander?"

"No gun, remember?"

"I forgot."

"That's why you're a lieutenant and I'm a commander." He turned to deal with some paperwork. Stobbs stopped at the door.

"One more question."

"Shoot."

"What about Ridzik?"

Ridzik, thought Donnelly, always Ridzik. Personally, he liked Art, but sometimes he thought it might be better if Ridzik wasn't a cop; or if he had to remain one, let him be one someplace else. "Art is a good cop."

"He's also a master at fucking up."

"That too," agreed Donnelly. "So if he fucks up, good-bye Art. Departmentally speaking, I got no downside here."

"We'll see," said Stobbs.

Ridzik and Danko were ploughing through the crowds of people in the booking hall like icebreakers, heading toward an interrogation room.

"I brought in Gallagher's snitch," Ridzik explained. "I figure if we lean on him hard enough . . ."

"Snitch?"

"You know, informer."

"Yes."

"He gave us a bust we made the other day. Cleanheads."

"Negroes without hair."

"That's one way of putting it. He's sleazy as hell, but if we can get him to talk, I got a feeling he'll be able to tell us who's brokering the Cleanhead deal."

"He is one of the men who visit Viktor in jail. Yes?"

"No." Ridzik looked at the slip of paper he had been given by Gloria. "Viktor only had two visitors. One was some skirt named Cat Manzetti. The other was the guy I shot. His name is Tatamovitch or something like that."

Danko nodded. He knew the name. Tatamovitch. Another Georgian. And he was wanted for murder, blackmail, and pimping. Danko added him to the list of people who would understand Soviet justice when all this was done.

"Who is the woman?"

"She's a teacher. Teaches dance in Wicker Park—you don't know where that is, but it isn't the greatest of neighborhoods. Self-help bullshit, that's what she teaches, basically. We'll try and catch up with her tonight."

They stopped at the institutional gray door of the interrogation room, and stared through the little window at Streak, Gallagher's informer. The young black man leaned back in his chair as if he didn't have a care in the world. He was a pretty big guy, and pretty tough too, as long as he didn't have to deal with anything more heavyweight than recalcitrant hookers or old lady shopkeepers who didn't really want to pay for the "protection" Streak offered them. He did okay financially. He was wearing a pretty loud Italian silk suit that didn't really appeal to Ridzik, but he guessed he had to pay at least eight long for it.

Art Ridzik turned to Danko. "Now look," he said, like a quarterback giving instructions in a huddle, "this is America. In this country we protect the rights of individuals, even the rights of part-time pimp piles of shit like him." He jerked a thumb over his shoulder. "It's a law called Miranda."

"You name your laws after women?"

"Shuttup and listen. Miranda says you can't touch his ass."

Danko's eyes narrowed. Who was this Miranda? "I don't want to touch his ass. I want to make him talk."

Ridzik exhaled heavily. "Look, I'm going to handle this, okay?"

"Does he know where is Viktor?"

"Maybe."

"Good."

Ridzik opened the heavy door and walked into the room. He sat down in a chair across the table from Streak. The room, he noted, had all the charm of a subway car.

Streak launched himself across the scored and cigarette-burnt table. "Hey, dickweed," he yelped, "what the fuck is this shit? What kind of asshole are you anyway? You are some kind of fuckin'—"

Danko could not quite believe his ears. A criminal, a pimp at that, was talking to a police officer like this. Of all the bewildering and completely incomprehensible things he had heard and seen since being in America, this was the strangest? No. The strangest things was that Ridzik didn't seem to think that this kind of behavior was strange at all. Streak continued to shriek.

"You got nothing on me. This is *buuul*shit. And you know it, cocksucker."

Danko had had enough, even if Ridzik hadn't. He stepped behind Streak, yanked him up, twisted his arm behind his back, and slammed the pimp into the concrete wall. Ridzik winced.

"Where is Viktor?" bellowed Danko in Streak's ear.

Ridzik did his best to separate the two men. "Danko? What the fuck—"

Danko tightened his grasp on Streak's arm. The man screamed in pain. Ridzik tried to pry loose Danko's grasp. All they needed was a prisoner with a broken arm. That would open an incredible can of worms. Ridzik jammed himself between the two men and managed to push Danko off the hapless pimp.

"Be civilized," said Ridzik. Danko glared at him, not sure if he should deck Ridzik or Streak first. "C'mon, Danko, this is my town. I know how things are done here."

Ivan Danko took a step back. Fine, he thought, we'll see how the American methods worked. He could always resort to his own procedures later, if things didn't work out the way Ridzik seemed to think they would.

Art pushed Streak back into his chair. The pimp nursed his injured arm. "I don't know who the fuck he thinks he is," he whined, "but I'm gonna have both your badges for brutality."

"Hey, Streak, Streak, my man, calm down," said Ridzik soothingly. "We just want to ask you a few questions. Forget my pal here—too much caffeine, you know how it is. We just want you to fill us in a little on the Cleanhead action."

"Fuck you," spat Streak.

"That's not nice, Streak. Sergeant Ridzik is going to get mad."

"Like I give a shit. I told you, I told Gallagher everything I know."

Ridzik rubbed his hands together. He slipped his wallet out of his back pocket, extracted a crisp fifty from a wad of bills and folded it neatly, all the while smiling at Danko, like a magician performing a particularly complicated trick. Danko, for his part, just stared, unbelieving, at the American policeman. He was *paying* the prisoner for information. Never in his life had he heard of such stupidity. Danko knew a quicker, more effective, *cheaper* way of getting this man to talk.

Ridzik slipped the folded fifty into the breast pocket of Streak's jacket. The pimp smiled.

"A fair price for services rendered. Capitalism works, right, Streak?"

"That's what makes this country great."

"So render some services."

Streak smirked, smug. "Cleanheads got a monster deal goin' down. I told Gallagher. End of story." He folded his arms across his chest and leaned back in his chair as if to say, "Your move, copper."

"He lies," said Danko.

Ridzik looked resigned. "Well, you see, in this country he got the God-given right to do that." Ridzik sighed. "Oh well, easy come, easy go."

"Speakin' of goin', officer, when do I get sprung?"

"Well, Mr. Streak, seeing as we got nothing to hold you on . . ."

"That's right."

"So—" Ridzik stopped, frowned, and sniffed the air like a bird dog. "Hey, Danko, you smell something?"

"Criminal," said Danko, "hooligan."

"No," said Ridzik, "something else. Real familiar."

"Yo, Ridzik, what is this shit?"

"Yeah," said Ridzik, recognition flooding his face. "I know what that is. I smell heroin. Yeah, smack and real strong."

Streak jumped to his feet. "What is this bullshit?"

Ridzik reached into Streak's breast pocket and pulled out a small plastic envelope of whitish yellow powder. "Ohmigod, Streak," he said like a worried parent, "did you bring this in here? You brought this shit into a police station?"

Streak was screaming now. "Wait a fucking minute! You planted that shit!"

Ridzik was shaking his head. "This is serious, man. Very serious. You bein' on parole and everything. This is very bad for you, Streak." Ridzik clicked his tongue. "Three-to-five mandatory. And you see, Danko, they'll kill him as soon as he's in the population, him being a snitch. They hate informers inside. They make life—and death—very unpleasant. Ain't that so, Streak?"

Streak was bouncing off the walls. "This is a fucking cop setup. Bullshit, man, bullshit." He pointed at Ridzik as if is index finger were a stiletto. "You are fired. You might as well go an' clean out your desk because you are off the force, asshole. You know who I got on retainer? I gotta lawyer—"

"Cleanhead deal, Streak," pressed Ridzik. "Who, when, and where?"

"Lawyer I got makes the ACLU look like Nazis, man. He lives for cop fuckin' misconduct. He'll prob'ly sue your mangy ass for free. I ain't telling you shit. You hear me? *Shit!*"

Danko shook his head. They had tried Ridzik's way. Now they would try Soviet method. He leaped out of his chair, grabbed Streak's arm, whipped him around as if he was dancing with him, cinched the arm up tight against the snitch's back and then slammed the man face first into the concrete wall.

"Planting and police brutality," he said, his mouth jammed up against the cinder block.

Brutality? thought Danko. This wasn't brutality. *This* is brutality. Danko's hand closed over one of Streak's ringed fingers. He squeezed, the finger cracked.

"Sonovabitch!" screamed the pimp.

Another finger crunched. It sounded like someone cracking a lobster claw in a seafood restaurant. "Jesus! Okay! Okay!" Streak talked fast. "Abdul Elijah's running the deal from Joliet. Shit's coming in a couple of days. I don't know where." He felt Danko's hand closing over another finger. Streak's voice jumped an octave in fear and pain. "Swear on my balls, man, I don't know where."

"He doesn't know," said Ridzik.

Danko released Streak. The man buried his injured paw in his stomach and slid down the wall, groaning and cussing.

"Abdul?"

"Oh, you're just gonna love him, comrade," said Ridzik.

"We go."

"Hey, Streak," said Ridzik bending over the man and taking back his fifty. "Like the man says, we go. And look, I'm really sorry about your hand, catching it in the door like that." He patted the man lightly on the shoulder. "You gotta be more careful, my man."

Chapter Six

In the long ride to the prison, Ridzik filled
Danko in on Brother Abdul Elijah. He told the
story matter-of-factly, as if it was just a part of
police life, but to Danko it sounded like the
strangest tale he had ever heard.

"Elijah's a big time-crook, head of one of the
biggest criminal organizations going."

"But now he's in jail, he is nobody."

Ridzik shook his head. "Not quite, not quite."

"But he's in prison?"

Ridzik took his eyes off the road long enough
to glance at Danko. "Yeah, he's inside. We
occasionally make an arrest over here, you
know."

"I am glad to hear it. I have been taught
that your country was totally lawless and run
by gangsters. Tell me about Miranda."

Ridzik leaned on the horn of the car, urging
the car ahead of him to take advantage of the
green light. Quickly. "Miranda." He took his
hands off the wheel for a moment. "What can I
tell you. Basically, it's a good law. It's designed

to protect the innocent. But it cuts both ways, you know? It also gives scumbags the right to keep their mouths shut until some scumbag lawyer shows up and tells the first scumbag what to say."

Danko didn't need a translation of the word *scumbag,* even though it had not been taught at Kiev. "In Soviet Union you have right to speak to a lawyer, too."

That surprised Ridzik. "No kidding?"

"After two days in custody."

"Two *days?* Are you shitting me?"

"I am not shitting you."

"Man," said Ridzik, "you guys got it wired. I mean, we're supposed to uphold the law but that doesn't mean the law is on our side. You know what I mean?"

It was yet another weird side to American law enforcement. "No."

Ridzik put a cigarette in his mouth but just before flicking his lighter he shot a sideways glance at his passenger. "That suit is not going to explode or anything is it?"

"I think you are safe."

Hey, thought Ridzik, that was almost a joke. "Just checkin'," he said.

Danko thought that Joliet was not bad as prisons went. As they walked behind two guards, he glimpsed the cells, which seemed to him to be spacious and airy with only six beds in each. Some, he was amazed to see, had televison sets, in color yet. Prisoners lolled around on the galleries, talking or listening to music or idly clipping through magazines. It was further proof that the Americans were soft on their hooligans. Prison was not supposed to be so luxurious —no wonder it held no terrors for the criminals.

"This man Abdul sells drugs from prison? How is that possible?"

"Simple. Once we lock these guys up, the gangs take over. They run the joint."

"But the guards—"

"They got the keys, but they don't have the clout. I mean, it's about five or six to one. There are parts of the prison that are off limits to the COs." He gestured down the hallway. "I mean, would you go down there?"

"Yes."

Ridzik nodded. "I guess I could have figured that.

"The gangs run the place. Aryan Brotherhood, Mexican Mafia, Cleanheads, El Rukns, Muslims—they run the population the way governments, a lot of governments, run their countries—terror. And since most convicts are repeaters, the leader of the gang has a lot of outside connections."

The guard unlocked a gate. To his astonishment, Danko found himself in a gymnasium, a well-equipped one too. Much better than the army facilities. There was a weight-lifting area, a basketball court, weight machines where convicts were working out vigorously. The room was large enough for groups of men to toss footballs and baseballs back and forth.

"Cleanhead playground," said the guard. "From here on in, you're on your own." The gate clanged shut behind them.

"Listen," said Ridzik, "if you hear any screams—"

"Don't worry," said the CO. "We'll call the police."

"I feel much better."

Danko continued to stare around the room. On the weight-lifting stage stood an enormous black, bald lifter. He was struggling with what looked like a 159-kilo weight. The bar was at his chest. The man took a deep breath and, with tremendous effort, jerked the weight over his head, screaming from the exertion of it. A small number of Cleanheads clapped and whistled.

"All right, ma man," said one.

"That man is exercising," said Danko. He made *exercising* sound like the strangest thing he had ever heard of.

"Beautiful, isn't it? We don't starve 'em to death here like in Siberia. We feed 'em good, let 'em work out, lift weights. When they come in here they're bad motherfuckers. When they get out they're big, strong, healthy, bad mother-fuckers." Gradually, activity in the gym stopped as the presence of outsiders—white, cop outsiders—registered. Ridzik felt his stomach lurch. "Hi, kids. Just go on playing."

"What the fuck you want, man?" yelled one of them.

In the far corner of the room sat a small, wiry man. He had a full head of hair and a well-tended short beard. He wore mirrored sunglasses. He hadn't even looked in the direction of the two cops, but he seemed to know they were there. He smiled, as if to himself. Ridzik thought he looked like a very cool jazz musician.

"That's him, Abdul Elijah. You'll notice he has hair. He makes his followers shave their heads to prove their obedience but I guess he doesn't have to prove anything to himself. The rules are always different for the man at the top, right, Ivan? Kind of like back home in Russia."

"We talk to him."

"Not yet. Hey," Ridzik shouted, pointing at a Cleanhead near him. "C'mere."

The young, powerfully built man ambled over. "What?"

"This is Captain Danko. He's come all the way from Russia to talk to your scoutmaster there."

"Who the fuck are you?"

Ridzik felt himself getting mad. "Who the fuck am I? Who the fuck are you? I'm the tooth fairy, asshole. Go get your boss."

"Brother Abdul Elijah got no interest in talking to the man."

"Lemme hear it from him, shithead. Move your ass."

The Cleanhead wandered over to Abdul, taking his time, as if Ridzik and Danko weren't there. Art Ridzik shook his head; these people were pissing him off.

"These men have no respect for our authority as police officers," observed Danko.

"Jeez, how do you figure that?"

Danko advanced a few steps into the room, paused, and then walked over to the weight rack. He bent down and seized the bar that the bald lifter had had so much trouble with. He tugged on it as if testing its weight.

"C'mon," said Ridzik. "Don't get crazy with that thing. That thing must weigh three hundred pounds."

"One fifty-nine."

"Bullshit."

"Kiloes—2.2 pounds to the kilo."

Ridzik did some fast math. "Then it weighs 350 pounds. You want to get a—"

Danko snapped the weight cleanly to his chest and then, as if he were playing with a child, hefted the bar quickly up above his head.

"—hernia?" Ridzik finished.

Danko straightened his back. A perfect military press. He held the weight high and firm, not even working up a sweat. He turned slowly as if he were in competition, a full circle, letting the Cleanheads get a good look. There was some murmuring from the crowd. Danko strode across the room toward Abdul Elijah, as if he were no more encumbered than by a moderately heavy suitcase. Impassively, he looked at the Cleanhead leader, looking at his own reflection in Abdul Elijah's mirrored shades, then dropped the weight with a thundering crash at the man's feet. Cleanheads scattered but Abdul didn't flinch. The sound of the weight hitting the floor rolled through the big room like far-off thunder.

"Danko. People's Militia, Moscow Division."

"Talk to my secretary. Maybe I can squeeze you in." Abdul walked away.

"Secretary?"

"Yeah," said one of the Cleanheads with an ugly smile. "You can ask him for an appointment."

"Him" was a giant black man dressed in filthy prison blues. He was advancing slowly on Danko, looking mean. To Ridzik, the secretary looked like a locomotive in overalls.

Danko nodded. He had to fight the man for the privilege of speaking to Abdul Elijah, a prisoner. He wondered just how many strange things he would see and learn about today. He walked back to Ridzik, taking off his suit jacket as he went.

"This is new suit. Please hold coat for me."

"Oh c'mon, Danko, you aren't really going to fight him, are you?"

Danko shrugged. "It is childish, but if they insist . . ." He unbuttoned the cuffs of his shirt and rolled them back. "I will win."

Ridzik looked at Danko and then over at Abdul's secretary. "Bullshit. This guy is huge. Suppose you don't?"

"Then the guards will have to shoot him."

"Oh yeah, right."

Jamal stood in the middle of a ring of clapping, catcalling Cleanheads. He flexed his muscles and chopped his hands in the air and kicked, letting Danko know he had some experience in martial arts.

Ridzik watched him, feeling a little sick to his stomach. From across the room he could feel the awesome power of the man. Danko might be strong and tough but this was going to be a little more than he could handle. Ridzik knew it for sure when Danko stepped up to his adversary with his fists extended in a stance reminiscent of Jim Corbett. His fists were far out in front of him, his chin up, as if inviting a pulverizing blow. Swell, thought Ridzik, the Commissar of Queensbury rules. He almost couldn't watch.

The Cleanheads were delighted. Jamal advanced on Danko, who stood stiff and awkward waiting for him. The Cleanhead's moves were fluid and graceful, his muscles rippling powerfully. "Hey, Gentleman Jim, that how you fight?" he taunted.

Danko looked puzzled and lowered his fists. "Maybe it is better we fight Russian rules."

"How's that?"

Danko demonstrated. The secretary never saw the kick coming, but he certainly felt its effects. Danko's foot slammed into the man's crotch, mashing his balls. Jamal screamed and doubled over in pain, his shriek echoing in the gym. Danko stepped up and punched him once, an economical blow that carried the power of a runaway truck. Jamal dropped as if he had been shot.

There was silence in the gym as Danko walked back to Ridzik. He rebuttoned his cuffs and slipped on his jacket. "Now I talk to Abdul."

"Glad I could bring you two together."

Three Cleanheads dragged the secretary across the gym floor, hauling him back to the cage. Danko passed them, glancing at the unconscious man the way people look at traffic accidents they slowly pass on the road.

Abdul Elijah had not reacted during the fight. He did not react now that Danko stood towering over him.

"Why do you keep that man in the hole?" asked Danko as the metal bars clanged down over the cage.

"My secretary?" said Abdul Elijah softly. "He had impure thoughts. I am teaching him self-control."

"Soviet schools teach history of American Negro and his struggle for liberation. What was your political crime?" It was the best Danko could do for the "good cop" approach.

"I robbed a bank. Now what do you want, Mr. Moscow? Get to it."

"I have Viktor's key."

Abdul Elijah remained impassive. "If that's true, then you have Viktor's money. Now, all you need is half a one-hundred dollar bill, and you and me, we're in business."

"I give you key. You give me Viktor." Danko pulled the key out of his inside pocket, carefully shielding it from Ridzik's line of sight. Abdul thought for a moment.

"It ain't ethical," he said finally.

"You keep the cocaine."

Abdul shook his head slowly. "You're asking me to compromise my ethics, my principles. That drug is a political tool, you understand, the money is just a means to a political end."

"And you'll do what?"

"I am going to destroy your country, white boy. The two great powers, America and the Soviet Union, will drown in drugs. They will kill you both."

It was all Danko could do to stop himself reaching out and strangling the slightly built man. "We are not American police," he said quietly, his voice heavy with menace. "You send drugs to my country and one day you wake up and find your testicles floating in a glass of water next to your bed."

"I'm a holy man. Got no need for testicles."

"Then we settle for your eyes."

Abdul smiled and raised his glasses. His eyes were sightless and staring. There were scars on either side of them, a reminder of a badly built homemade bomb that had gone off when it wasn't supposed to. He dropped the glasses back over his eyes.

"You can't threaten me, white boy."

"Then we kill you."

The smile never left Abdul's face. "I'm thirty-eight years old and I been behind bars for twenty-six of 'em. Killing me doesn't hurt. It sets me free, man."

"You are not free to destroy my country."

Abdul Elijah shook his head slowly. "You just don't understand, do you, man? This country, the USA, was built on exploiting the black man. I don't hear about brothers in your country, white boy—"

There were black men in Russia, thought Danko, students from Third World countries. Twice he had investigated crimes against them —young men who had been beaten up by Russians because they had gone out with white girls.

"—but you exploit your own people. Make them slaves. I guess that makes me the only Marxist in the room, *comrade*," he said stressing the word ironically, "and you're nothing but another lackey for the man."

"I am police officer."

"You are a servant." Abdul shifted his weight. "See, you just don't understand. This ain't a drug deal. This is spiritual. I'd like to sell drugs to every white man in the world. And his sister."

Danko stared at him for a long minute. He could hear every sound in the gym, could hear Abdul breathing and the mocking silence between them. Danko did not care about politics, he did not care about this black man. He cared about revenge.

"I want Viktor Rosta."

Abdul Elijah nodded. "Yeah. Real bad. I can feel you want him *real* bad."

"Where do I find him?" He felt his anger level rising again. He wondered if it would do any good to hit Abdul. Doubtless, that would bring the other Cleanheads to the rescue and Danko was not sure he could handle them all. Ridzik would help, probably. Ivan Danko reminded himself that he had his gun for defense, but he was sure that if he shot an American prisoner, even in self-defense, it would slow down his search for Viktor.

"Tell you what I'm gonna do, white boy. I'm gonna see if I can put you together with Viktor."

"When?"

"Hold on now. I'll fix it. I'll put you together with him and we'll see if we can work this thing out. Cause I need Viktor, and Viktor, he need the key. And you"—he smiled again—"you, comrade, are just one more motherfucker we got to deal with."

"How? How will you arrange this thing from prison?"

"I can arrange anything I want from the joint, Mr. Moscow," Abdul Elijah started to drift away. "Be cool."

Danko watched him go.

He was silent for most of the ride back to Chicago, trying to decide what to tell Ridzik. He decided to tell him nothing. If Abdul Elijah arranged a meeting with Viktor, Danko wanted to take it alone. He would not need Ridzik.

Art Ridzik had decided he could play the great stone face as well as Danko. He didn't ask any questions, but as the car ate up the miles he found his curiosity craving to be satisfied. Finally he broke down.

"Well, you gonna tell me how it went?"

"It went fine."

Ridzik pounded the wheel in frustration. "Come on, cut that shit. You were with that fucker so long I was thinking of getting my head shaved myself."

"Could be good idea," Danko said. Just then, the beeper on Danko's watch went off. He snapped down the stem and the beeping stopped.

"What the hell is that?"

"My watch. I leave it on Moscow time."

"Yeah? What time is it back there? Time to get up?"

Danko shook his head. "Time to feed my parakeet."

"Oh." They drove a mile in silence. "Feed your parakeet. What is that? Russian for jerking off?"

Danko looked sternly at Ridzik and shook his head.

"No, I guess not."

Another mile passed. "Is there something wrong with parakeet?"

Ridzik was absolutely sure that Ivan Danko was the strangest character he had ever met in his life, even weirder than a kid he knew in high school who used to eat bugs and spend a lot of time in the basement of his house with his chemistry set.

"Hey, no. Nothing wrong with parakeets. I got nothing against them. My kid sister used to have one. You want to have a parakeet, that's just fine with me."

"You think parakeet is feminine."

"Feminine?"

"You say your sister had one."

"No, it's not feminine. I mean, it's not quite having a pit bull, but it's not having a chihuahua either. I mean, what do I know. I guess it's okay."

Danko nodded relieved. "Thank you."

"You're welcome." Ridzik wondered if these days were as long as he thought they were, or was it just his imagination.

Chapter Seven

But the day wasn't over yet. Danko insisted—
and Ridzik wanted to anyway—on going to
interview the woman, the dance teacher who
had visited Viktor Rosta in prison. As Art Ridzik
guided the car toward Wicker Park, he decided
that first he had to lay down some rules with
Danko. He hadn't liked being squeezed out of
the action at the prison—he wasn't sure he
would have fought the secretary or some other
hard guy for the privilege, but he figured that
Danko at least should have shared the information he got.

He pulled the car to the curb in front of the
address. It was a shabby old commercial building with a dry cleaners and a liquor store on
the street floor. On the second story were lighted
windows. DANCE STUDIO had been inexpertly
lettered on them.

"This is it. Now listen, Danko, I run the
cross-examinations, okay? That way, we avoid
these private non-Ridzik conversations between
you and suspects. Dig?"

"Dig?"

Ridzik chuckled. "What's the matter? Don't they teach you *dig* at Kiev?"

"Holes?"

"Forget it."

They climbed the sagging stairs to the second floor of the building, the sound of recorded music getting louder. For a moment, Danko was reminded of the day he and Yuri had climbed the stairs to Viktor's den months before in Moscow. If he had not made a mistake that day he would not be here now—and Viktor would have received his richly deserved punishment.

Ridzik pushed on the door of the studio. It was a fairly large room with a worn hardwood floor. There were mirrors and ballet barres on one wall. A dark-haired woman in a leotard and leg warmers leaned against one of the barres, smoking a cigarette and watching a dozen or so teenage girls going through their dance motions. Ridzik thought she looked like someone he might want to get to know a little better. She looked great in tights: her breasts pushed against the elastic fabric, which clung tightly to shapely legs and a fine ass.

"That's good," she yelled. "Keep going." She flicked away a long ash on her cigarette. "Don't slink, Deenecia—this isn't a strip bar. Bolt that butt down."

One of the girls tucked in her ass and caught the rhythm of the music.

"That's better," said the instructor. Then she glanced at the door, saw Ridzik and Danko, and her attitude of bored competence changed. Danko nodded. It was the woman from the hotel.

The tape ran out. "Okay, class," she yelled. "Start the tape over and go through the motions again." She walked over to the two policemen.

"Brought a cop with you this time," she said, jerking her head toward Ridzik.

"That's good. How can you tell?"

"Practice."

"You left the hotel without paying your bill," said Danko.

"Yeah, I was in a hurry." She flicked some more ash. "Nice suit."

It clicked with Ridzik. This was the chick Danko saw taking a shower, or something, at the Garvin. "This is beautiful. I love it when old friends meet up again."

"Viktor's girl," said Danko.

Cat Manzetti hesitated a moment, then walked past them into the cramped little room that served as her office. There was a beat-up desk, a telephone, and a grimy window. An untidy stack of tapes stood on the desk. She slumped behind the desk and took a deep drag on her cigarette.

"Why don't you show me some ID?—I like to know who I'm talking to."

Ridzik flashed his badge. "Ridzik, Arthur. This is Captain Danko, from Moscow."

"No shit. You're a long way from home."

"You went to see Viktor Rosta in jail."

Cat let the smoke trail out of her mouth. "Yeah. So? He asked me to."

"What'd you talk about?" asked Ridzik.

"The weather, taxes, inflation," she said lightly.

"You meet him hanging around hotel bars? Or do you work the lobbies?"

Cat's face darkened in anger. "Fuck you. You got something to arrest me for, then do it. But I don't have to listen to this shit." She started from the room, heading back into the studio. Danko grabbed her arm.

"Let me go, you fuckin' Russian bastard." She twisted under Danko's grasp, but he held on. He wasn't hurting her, but as long as he had hold of her, she wasn't going anywhere either. He looked into her eyes; there was something in his expression that told her he had no intention of hurting her. She stopped struggling.

"Just what do you want with me, anyway?" she asked plaintively. The tough act was gone.

"What did you bring Viktor from the hotel? It is very important. Many people could be hurt." He released his hold on her arm.

Cat Manzetti touched the spot where he had held her. Ridzik couldn't quite believe his eyes. This Danko, the same guy who had broken two of Streak's fingers as if they were breadsticks and had decked a Cleanhead without working up a sweat, had turned into Mr. Nice.

"Look," said Cat slowly, "I don't want any trouble. Viktor told me to go to the Garvin, get his old room. He told me where to look."

"And what did you find?"

Cat shrugged. "A passport and half a hundred-dollar bill."

Danko nodded. Abdul Elijah had mentioned half of a bill. With that, he had said, they would be in business.

Of course, Ridzik knew nothing about it. The passport interested him more. If Rosta made a break for it, managed to get out of the country, then he just might be beyond the reach of the Chicago Police Department.

"Fake passport?" Ridzik asked.

"Real passport," Danko said, "fake name."

"You know more about it than I do," said Cat. "I didn't look."

"What did you do with it?"

"I gave it to Viktor's friend."

"Who?" demanded Ridzik.

"I don't know his name."

"Convenient."

"It's the truth."

Ridzik frowned in annoyance. "Bullshit, lady. Cut the crap, would ya? Where is he?"

Cat met tough with tough. The bewildered, slightly scared woman of a moment before vanished. "I told you, I don't know."

"Got a phone number?" Ridzik moved in close, crowding her. She stood her ground.

"I lost it."

"Viktor is a very bad guy."

She stubbed out her cigarette. "Really?"

"Because of him a cop died."

"I don't know anything about that," she said in a "I don't give a shit" voice. But she did. She knew Viktor Rosta and she knew that he was more than capable of killing a cop. This whole thing was getting a little too heavy for her liking.

Ridzik was mad now. "Look, lady, the rate you're goin'—all I'm saying is that when Viktor goes down you go with him."

Cat turned her big brown eyes on him, holding them wide with feigned innocence and fear. "Oooo, is the big tough policeman trying to scare me into helping him?"

"I'm trying to figure out why the fuck you want to help a dirty—"

"He's my husband," she said shortly. Then she turned on her heel and walked back into the studio, just as the music stopped.

"Husband?" said Ridzik. He felt his blood pressure soar. "I am going to bust this bitch so hard she bounces." He started after her.

Danko stood in his way. "We must use her."

"Bullshit! We'll use her, but in an interrogation room down at the station. That's where we'll use her."

Danko was thinking moves ahead, like a chess player. "If she remains free, she will lead us to Viktor. I believe now she does not know where he is."

Ridzik scowled. "You must be the ESP detective I hear so much about."

Then Danko did something that was, for Danko, pretty strange. He put his hand on Ridzik's shoulder. "Please," he said, "trust me."

On the way back to the car, Danko sketched in the new information. He knew why Viktor had married this woman. "For travel visa to the United States. In Soviet Union it is much easier to leave the country if you are married to a foreign national. But she will lead us to him, I am sure of it. Or perhaps he will come to me."

"Come to you? I'da thought you are about the last person he would want to run into."

"Perhaps."

Ridzik's eyes narrowed and he took a long look at Danko. "You know," he said, "I'm beginning to get the idea that there's a little more to this than Captain Danko doing his duty to the Fatherland."

"Motherland. Soviet Union is Motherland."

"Whatever. Square with me, comrade, there's something personal between you two, isn't there? Rosta might want the drugs, but he wants you too, right? And you want to stop the drugs, but most of all you want Rosta."

Danko nodded.

"So?"

"Six months ago I shot his brother. In Moscow."

"Shot him dead?" Just winging him didn't count much to Ridzik.

"Yes."

"Hey, not bad. Way to go." It was the best piece of news he had heard all day.

"Thank you." Danko walked a few more yards toward the car, then stopped. "He killed my partner," he said in a low voice.

Ridzik shook his head. Russians, Americans —it didn't matter. Cops were cops and a dead partner was bad news no matter which side of the border you happened to be on. "I'm sorry to hear that, really."

"Thank you."

"So, Danko, you and me, we finally got something in common. Viktor killed my partner. That means we both have an interest in nailing his ass."

Danko nodded. "This girl will lead us to him."

Ridzik glanced up at the dance studio windows. The music had stopped and some of the lights were out. A few of the dance students were coming down the stairs and crowding out into the street. It looked like the two cops were going to be running a little surveillance that night. Ridzik glanced across the street to a diner.

"A good cop is never wet and never hungry. It ain't raining, but I could use a little something to eat. As long as we're here, we might as well score some food."

Danko was not interested in eating.

Ridzik gestured toward the diner. "Over there you got your four major food groups: hamburger, fries, coffee, and doughnuts."

"Doughnuts?"

"You'll love 'em. Meet you in the car." Ridzik started to cross the street.

"Wait," called Danko.

"Don't tell me: extra mayo, no onions, side of borscht."

"Give me the key to the car."

"It's not locked."

Danko glanced toward the dance studio windows. "In case she leaves."

Ridzik shook his head. "You can't drive that car. It's regulations. Something happens, you crack up, God forbid hit a law-abiding citizen or his car, Danko, I'll be doing paperwork until I retire. Forget it."

"If she takes a taxi cab," explained Danko patiently, "I'm not sure I can run fast enough to follow her."

Ridzik stared. Why hadn't he listened to his old man and become an accountant? "You'd try, too, wouldn't you?"

"Yes."

"Oh, fuck it." He tossed the keys to the Russian, praying as he did so that Manzetti managed to stay put long enough for the diner to provide him with a couple of cheeseburgers.

Danko slid behind the wheel and put the key in the ignition. He glanced at the instruments on the dashboard. Cars were cars. He did not think he would have any more trouble driving this Chevy than his Lada back in the USSR. From his inside pocket he took the key and a cheap steel ballpoint pen. He rummaged around in the trash on the floor of the car, found an unstained napkin, and carefully copied down the manufacturer's serial number of the key. That done, he turned his eyes on the entrance of the dance studio, and did not look away.

At least, he didn't until he heard a voice growling at him through the passenger's window. Glowering at him through the window was a big man, big from fat, not from muscles, with a three-day growth of beard and a mean look in his eye. In one ham fist he held a bottle

of beer, in the other, a baseball bat. He did not
look happy. Danko glanced at the man and
saw that he was wearing a grimy T-shirt with
Chicago Bears emblazoned across the front.
Danko wondered if the Chicago Bears were
another street gang, like the Cleanheads. The
man took a deep swig from the beer bottle,
belched, and rested a beefy forearm on the
ledge of the window.

"Hey, asshole, you can't park here." The Bears
fan got a good look at Danko's suit and figured
him to be one of those missionaries, maybe a
Jehovah's Witness or a Mormon—a nice Jesus-
loving kid who would cause no trouble.

Danko looked puzzled. "Why not?"

"This is my parking space," growled the man.
"I live right up there"—he waved the baseball
bat vaguely—"so move your piece of shit car
the hell out of my space." He let Danko get a
good look at the baseball bat. *"Or* you can
gimme fifty bucks," he said, as if he was being
a real nice guy and giving the kid a break.

"I don't understand."

"Look," said the man, exhaling a wave of
beer fumes into the car, "I'm gonna make this
real simple. It's like this: move your ass or pay
me fifty; or I take my Pete Rose here and
fucking mutilate your car."

This man was distracting Danko from his
purpose. He glanced back at the doorway of
Cat Manzetti's building. Another light had gone
out upstairs. She was definitely preparing to
leave.

"Hey, did you fuckin' hear me?"

Danko did not take his eyes off the building. "Go away."

"Sonovabitch!" screeched the guy. "You come into *my* neighborhood and tell *me* to get lost? I live here. This is my fucking parking place!" The guy was so mad that flecks of spittle flew from his mouth. "Now it's seventy-five bucks. Take a hike or I trash the car and fuck up your face for free."

Danko knew he was going to have to get rid of the man in order to go about his job in peace and quiet. But, he cautioned himself, he was in America and he was learning that he had to work by the American rules.

"Do you know Miranda?" he asked the man with the baseball bat.

"Huh? Never heard of the bitch."

Ah, thought Danko, that made everything all right. His fist flew off the steering wheel, catching the man squarely on the chin. The force of the blow seemed to lift him off his feet for a split second. He hung in the air, surprised, and then dropped out of sight, crumpling to the sidewalk. He didn't even groan.

Danko looked back at the dance studio, quietly pleased that he had dealt with a hooligan according to strict American methods.

Ridzik stepped over the guy as he got into the car. He glanced down at a Chicago citizen sprawled on the sidewalk in a puddle of blood and beer, then looked over at Danko. He was sure the Russian had something to do with it, but Ridzik didn't want to hear about it, then or ever. He put the two bags of take-out food on the seat between them.

"Everything okay?" he said, rooting around in the bags for his hamburger.

"Yes. Fine. No problems." Danko showed no interest in the food.

Ridzik couldn't resist. "What about that sack of shit lying on the sidewalk?" Little groans of pain were drifting up to the window as the man came round. Soon he would be wondering just what hit him—it couldn't have been the Mormon.

"He lives here."

Ridzik peered over the edge of the car window. The guy showed no signs of getting up. "Beautiful," he said. He looked back at Danko. "Do me a favor, avoid running over him when we take off."

"I will do my best."

"That's all we ask in the CPD. Here." He offered a cup of steaming hot coffee to Danko. Ridzik peeled off the container lid. "I don't know how you guys do it back in Moscow, but we always save the tops because if we have to move in a hurry . . ." Ridzik was balancing a cup of coffee and a burger, trying to get things organized. "Hey, and guess what? I called in to headquarters and they say the other Russian, the one I nailed—Tatamovitch—is coming out of his coma. Maybe we should bag this stakeout and go see if he—"

Danko tensed behind the wheel. "There she is."

She was standing in the shadow of the doorway, glancing nervously down the street. A yellow cab, nosing its way along the block, stopped directly in front of her. Danko saw her exchange a quick word with the driver, then hurriedly slip into the backseat. The cab slipped away from the curb, making good speed.

"Now we go," said Danko, twisting the key in the ignition. He slammed the car into gear and stomped on the accelerator, not quite prepared for the power of a Detroit engine. The car lurched forward.

As they took off, about half the steaming coffee in Ridzik's cup slopped over the edge into his lap.

"Jesus!" he screamed. "I just burnt my dick off!"

Danko didn't care. At last he was getting the chance to find Viktor. Ridzik's genitals were just another casualty in his private war. He pushed the car into traffic, keeping a few cars behind the cab.

"God damn!" bitched Ridzik, still cradling his crotch. "I ruined a suit and hard-boiled my balls. Who the fuck do I sue?" He was thrown against the side of the car as Danko pulled a tight right turn following the cab.

"You are one terrific driver," grumbled Ridzik.

"Please be quiet," said Danko.

"Please be careful with the goddamn car," yelled Ridzik. "I don't want any accidents," he said emphatically. "I'd have a year of paperwork to fill out."

"I have car under control." Danko stared straight ahead.

"Oh, sure," sneered Ridzik. "I guess they taught you all about crack-ups and the price of insurance at your famous school in Kiev."

"In socialist countries, insurance not necessary. State pays for everything."

Ridzik looked at Danko is disbelief. "Well, tell me something, Captain. If it's such a fuckin' paradise, how come everybody in your country's standing in line to get out?"

"Capitalist propaganda." Danko said it as if he believed it.

"And if you guys got it together so great, how come you're up the same creek as us with heroin and cocaine?"

"Is just beginning in Soviet Union. We will stop it." And they would.

"Good luck. It's like tryin' to hold back the ocean."

"The Chinese find way. Right after Revolution. They line up all drug dealers, all drug addicts, take them to public square—shoot them in back of head."

"Never work here. Fuckin' politicians wouldn't go for it."

"Shoot them first."

They followed the cab for at least fifteen minutes and not once did the driver of the cab make any attempt to lose them—he didn't even appear to have noticed he was being followed. Danko was not sure that was a good thing.

"Maybe she's just going home," said Ridzik, as if reading the Russian's mind.

Danko nodded, but it was not a possibility

he wanted to consider. He had come too far and endured too much to lose the case now.

"The hospital," said Ridzik, "that's where we ought to be headed. We should be there when that Tatamovitch wakes up from his nap."

"Not yet," said Danko, his eyes still glued to the taillights of the cab. He had to admit to himself that he enjoyed driving the car. It responded like a racehorse and he could feel the power of the engine under his fingers, which rested lightly on the wheel. It was not like his ornery underpowered Lada. He wondered how a policeman like Ridzik could afford a machine as luxurious as a Chevrolet—and he was sure that a man like Ridzik, for all his faults, was not the sort to take bribes.

Danko was in sufficient control of the car to follow the cab when it made a sudden and unexpected hard left into the dark mouth of a gaunt, gray underground parking garage. Danko felt his heart beat a little faster. The cab had tried to lose him and had failed. Now he was sure he was on his way to meet Viktor.

The Chevy glided down the ramp of the garage to the first level. There were rows and rows of cars parked there, each gleaming dully under the glare of the large overhead lights. The cab was not in sight. Danko brought the car to a halt, silently cursing himself for his stupid overconfidence.

"Lost him, comrade?" said Ridzik ironically.

On the far side of the garage, Danko saw the yellow roof of the cab and its lighted sign. It

was cruising along, headed for a ramp leading to
an even lower level.

"No," said Danko, easing the car forward.

As they headed down the ramp, the interior
of the cop's car was lit up by a pair of bright
headlights behind them.

"We are being followed," said Danko. "Cleanheads."

Ridzik twisted in his seat and looked. There
was a plain commercial van behind them, but
he couldn't see into the cab. He wondered how
Danko knew they were being followed by
Cleanheads—it was a pretty safe guess, Art
had to admit, but the Russian seemed so sure
about it.

"She set us up," Ridzik said.

It was now clear to Ivan Danko. He remembered the words of Abdul Elijah again: he would
find a way to bring him face-to-face with Viktor.
This was his way.

They were on the lower level now. It was a
vast concrete bunker, devoid of cars. There were
bright pools of light where the overheads shone
and, in stark contrast, areas of dark shadow.
Ridzik didn't like this at all. It was not a great
place for a shoot-out—but then, cops didn't usually get to choose where and when the shooting started.

Abruptly, Danko stopped the car and pulled
up the hand brake. The van stopped a few
yards behind them.

"Maybe we should abandon car."

Ridzik shook his head vehemently. "A Chicago cop does not abandon his car, no matter

what." He yanked his gun out of its holster. "Looks like things are going ballistic."

"No shooting," Danko said firmly, "Instead, we talk."

Ridzik glanced behind him. Cleanheads were jumping out of the van, each of them carrying an automatic weapon. He looked down sadly at his own gun. It didn't look like much compared to the firepower the Cleanheads had lined up. Reluctantly, he slid the gun back into the holster. He hoped the Cleanheads were in a talking mood.

The cab came out of the shadows and parked a few feet ahead of the cops. Shit, thought Ridzik. Cleanheads ahead of them, Cleanheads behind them. They were boxed in and outgunned. Not nice.

Danko took something out of his jacket pocket. "Hold this for me," he said, sliding his hand across the seat.

"What is it?"

"Viktor's key."

"I didn't even know you—"

"Just take."

Art Ridzik jammed the key into the pocket of his pants. The two cops got out of the car and stood in the harsh light. The Cleanheads behind them moved up a little, their weapons trained.

Cat Manzetti got out of the cab and started walking toward Ridzik and Danko. She was badly scared. Her "cab driver," another Cleanhead named Salim, had briefed and threatened her thoroughly on the ride from the studio to the garage. She had to deliver a message to the Russian cop, a message from Viktor. Then, if she was good and didn't fuck up, Salim would let her stay alive. Trembling slightly, she made her way across the garage.

"Whatever she's selling," whispered Ridzik, "don't buy it."

She stopped a few feet from Ridzik and Danko. Salim stationed himself a yard or two behind her, listening closely to what she said, making sure she got it right.

"I'm supposed to tell you," she said, her voice quavering with fear, "I'm supposed to say that this truce was arranged by someone named Abdul. You leave your guns with that guy over there." She shot a nervous glance over her shoulder at Salim.

"No way," said Ridzik. "Chicago cops don't give up their guns."

There was a series of harsh metallic scrapes as the Cleanheads behind Art chambered rounds in their automatics. He felt the hair on the back of his neck bristle. "They don't give up their weapons *unless* there's a really good reason."

Salim strode up to the two cops. "You got the key?" he asked Danko.

Again with this key, thought Ridzik. When the hell was someone going to let him into the secret of what the key opened?

Danko shook his head. "No."

"Where is it?"

"Safe place."

Ridzik had the key. He didn't feel like he

was in a safe place. It was nice of Danko to trust him with the thing that a bunch of heavily armed Cleanheads seemed very anxious to have.

"Maybe we better search you," said Salim, "just in case." He patted Danko's pockets, methodically searching for the key.

Ridzik did his best to keep his voice steady. "So what happens if you find it?"

"*Real* bad news."

Ridzik figured.

"Do you think I am so stupid I bring it with me?"

"No point in taking chances."

Ridzik looked closely at Salim, wondering if he had seen him before. He couldn't be sure, but he did know that he didn't like the look of the guy. He was— Hold it, thought Ridzik. This was one of the guys he had busted with Gallagher and Stobbs. He shook his head. Justice, he thought disgustedly.

Very slowly, Danko reached into his jacket. Ridzik could sense the Cleanheads behind him getting antsy. The Russian pulled out his gun and handed it to Salim. "You are wasting time. Where is Viktor?"

Salim seemed to lose interest in searching Danko. Ridzik remembered a few prayers he thought he had forgotten forever, pleading that the Cleanhead would decide not to search him either.

"He's over there," said Salim, nodding into the darkness.

"Great," said Art lightly. "Let's go talk to him. I'll be translator."

Salim took Ridzik's gun out of his shoulder holster, slipped back the hammer, and placed the barrel against Ridzik's temple. "You already got a job. You're the hostage."

"I always thought I'd make a good hostage," said Ridzik.

"Look," Cat said suddenly, her eyes still wide with fear. "I've done what you said. I'm outta here."

"Thanks a lot," said Ridzik sourly. "You've been a great help."

"Hey look, mister, I'm sorry, but this whole thing is way past me." She looked hopefully at Salim.

"Go." Cat Manzetti went, heading fast for the exit. Ridzik wished he were going with her, much as he hated the bitch. "Go see Viktor," said Salim to Danko, "but you get out of hand, Mr. Moscow, and your friend here is gonna be gone."

"Where is he?"

"Walk toward the light," Salim said, pointing. "He'll find you."

Danko started toward the pool of light in the middle of the room, his heavy footsteps echoing on the concrete floor. That and the far-off sound of an elevated train rushing by were the only sounds in the giant room. Just before Danko reached the spot, Viktor stepped out of the gloom. Danko kept walking until he was face-to-face with his enemy. For a long moment, the two men stared at one another. Danko fought the sudden urge to grab Viktor by the throat and choke the life out of him, no matter what the consequences.

An ironic smile played on Viktor's lips. He knew he held the upper hand. "We meet in strange places, Danko," he said in Russian.

"None of that Russian shit," said a voice. From the shadows came another Cleanhead. His gun was held level and firm. "Speak English. I gotta report on all this."

Viktor shrugged and took a pack of cigarettes from his inside pocket. He offered one to Danko, who didn't so much as move a muscle.

"If they let me have my gun, you would be dead, Danko." He struck a match, lit up, and inhaled. He tossed the match into the darkness.

"You think of me as some kind of lowlife," said Viktor, as if he were giving a lecture. "An outcast from society. I see myself as an agent for the people." He pointed with the cigarette. "Just like you."

Danko noted that Viktor spoke good English, better than his own. But no matter how well he said it, no words could mask his crimes.

"I do not sell drugs."

Viktor smiled as he exhaled. "The people have their needs. One is law and order"—he cocked his chin in Danko's direction—"the other is entertainment. I provide that."

"You provide poison."

Viktor drew some smoke deep into his lungs. "We are similar. We both respect courage. We both hold our own lives in contempt."

"You have contempt for all life."

What about the fucking key? thought the Cleanhead. What is this bullshit?

"You don't?" said Viktor. "You tell me you respect life? After all the blood you have shed?"

"You killed my friend."

"You killed my brother."

"Your brother was a criminal."

The two men glared at each other for a moment. Fresh hates welled within each as he remembered just how much the other had hurt him. In that moment, Viktor was prepared to forget the drug deal, the money, the power, forget everything for the pleasure of watching Ivan Danko die. But greed won out over revenge. He still needed the key, which meant he needed Danko. He shrugged.

"A dead man is a dead man. Brother, friend . . ." He flicked ash away, as if to show that the dead were of no use to him.

"Not to me."

"Perhaps not. But there are more important things at stake."

"Not to me."

"Business," muttered the Cleanhead, "talk business."

"He is right." Viktor inhaled again. "You have my key. I need it quite badly. I will pay for it. Generously. More than you will make in ten years."

Danko sneered with contempt. As long as Viktor Rosta cared more about money than revenge, Danko knew that he would win and Rosta would lose. "Kiss my ass."

Viktor stared icily at Danko. He knew that

he was going to have to find another way to get the key from Danko.

"You are so foolish, Captain. I had hoped that you might be more reasonable. Money has a way of making a man think clearly, but not in your case." He let the cigarette butt fall to the floor and ground it out. "Good night, Captain Danko," he said, walking back into the shadows.

The Cleanhead shook his head. This was no good at all. Brother Abdul would not like it.

"What about the girl?" Danko said suddenly.

Viktor stopped in his tracks and came halfway out of the shadows. "Are you telling me that sometimes a woman can succeed where money fails?" He studied Danko's face for a moment, then shook his head. "No, I don't think so. Not with you. You are the kind of Russian who looks forward only to death. I know your kind very well, Vanya. Remember, without me you do not exist."

"The girl," repeated Danko.

"She was useful. She made some of my time in this city enjoyable. Other than that, she is nothing. Take her if you like. As a gift."

Then he was gone.

Chapter Eight

The trouble was, Ridzik and Danko were still there. So were the Cleanheads. But something was going to happen, there was movement. The gun was still at Ridzik's head, but the other guys got back into the van. The engine started.

Carefully keeping the pistol on Danko, the Cleanhead walked him back to Ridzik.

"Where you been, bubba? I felt a little lonely here."

"Shuttup," said Salim. "They work it out?"

Danko's Cleanhead shook his head. "Nope."

Shit, thought Ridzik. He started looking around in his head for some kind of plan of action. If the Cleanheads decided to blow him away, he wasn't going to just stand there.

"Shit," said Salim. "Brother Abdul is going to be real unhappy. I'm tellin' you, Mr. Moscow, you are not giving us much of a choice."

Me neither, thought Ridzik.

"Choice?" said Danko.

"Yeah man, choice. Instead of just doing a

deal with Viktor, now we got to be on his side."
He lowered the gun from Ridzik's head. "You
hold out and we got to help him, we gotta fight
for him."

"You have another choice," said Danko.

"I don't think so, man."

"You could give Viktor to me. Forget him.
There will be other drug deals. American drug
deals."

"Well," said Ridzik, a little happier now that
he had some space between his head and the
barrel of a gun. "That's just fuckin' great. Nice
and cosy. Make a deal between the Russians
and the Cleanheads and leave the shit for us to
clean up."

The Cleanheads ignored Danko's deal and
Ridzik's vociferous objections to it. They started
getting into the van.

"I want my gun back," said Danko.

"Me too—"

The Cleanheads swung around, their weapons ready. For one sickening moment, Ridzik
was afraid they were going to start blasting.

"But you don't have to give it to me right
now. Look, mail me the gun. No sweat."

Salim smiled. "Don't worry, man. You guys
kept your word. So will we. Abdul is a man of
honor." He broke open the magazines of both
guns and scattered the bullets on the concrete
floor. They made a sound like metal hailstones.
The engine of the van roared into life and
zoomed across the deserted garage toward the
exit.

Ridzik waited for the reverberations to die

down a little, then picked up his gun and a couple of bullets. "I ought to kick your ass, you know." Ridzik spoke in a tone of almost normal conversation, as if he were saying, "I oughtta pick up a six on my way home," or "I wonder if there's anything good on TV tonight," but inside he was mad, seething mad.

"Try" was all Danko would say.

Ridzik had trouble controlling his anger and finally, once behind the wheel of his car, it came pouring out: "I don't give a shit that they gave us our guns back." He pressed hard on the gas and the car blasted up the ramp and out of the garage. "Those were the same guys who killed Gallagher." He was shouting now, his voice filling the car. "And you!" Danko loaded his gun, saying nothing. It was as if Ridzik wasn't even there. "You! You give me a fuckin' key, you don't tell me what it's for and it turns out everybody is ready to kill for it."

"It was a risk," Danko allowed.

"It wasn't *a* risk, shithead. It was *my* risk." Ridzik cut neatly into a stream of traffic headed downtown, ignoring the indignant horn blasts from the cars he had cut off. He slapped the wheel. "I don't know how you can even call yourself a cop, you know it? In this country we fucking trust our partners. We don't lie to 'em, we don't hold stuff back, and we absolutely do not leave them holding their dick while some hairless fuck shoves a gun in his ear." Ridzik took one hand off the wheel and dug something out of his pocket.

"Here." He slapped the key into Danko's hand. "You hold on to this in the future."

There was a moment of silence—silence except for Ridzik leaning on his horn to urge the car in front of him to move a little faster.

"I thought you could handle it," said Danko.

"What is that? Some kind of compliment?"

"Yes."

"Well, thank you, sir."

Either Danko didn't recognize the sarcasm or he chose to ignore it. "You are welcome."

Ridzik was calming down a little. "So what did you and Viktor talk about?"

Danko looked blankly at Ridzik, as if the Russian had suddenly forgotten his English. "Now we go see Tatamovitch at hospital."

Ridzik sighed. "You are a total shitheel, you know that?"

The first person they ran into at the hospital was Art Ridzik's old pal Nelligan. He was sitting in a little room off the Intensive Care Unit with a nice cup of coffee, a magazine or two, and an ashtray. He shared the room with a uniformed cop who seemed to be taking it just as easy. Through a window they could see a small ward. The first bed was occupied by Tatamovitch. Even the Russian seemed to be comfortable: carefully attending to him was a beautiful blond nurse. She was bent over his bed doing something that Ridzik couldn't see. But he did see her ass and he appreciated that.

"Hey, Ridzy," said Nelligan, putting down his copy of *People*.

Ridzik looked around at the cushy setup. "Jeez, you have it rough, Nelligan. I'da thought that after you turned me in they woulda made you head of homicide."

Nelligan put on his sincere face. "I do what I'm told to, Ridzy. And I keep the rules. That's what they're there for, right? Come on, no hard feelings, okay?"

Ridzik shot him a look that clearly translated as "fuck you" in any language. He turned to the uniform. "So what's up?"

"He started coming round about an hour or so ago."

"Said anything?"

"Mumbling in Russian."

"What did he say, in Russian," asked Danko.

"Russian isn't a requirement for my job, sir," said the uniform.

Score one for our side, thought Ridzik. "The nurse is in with him right now. We'll have a little chat with him as soon as she leaves."

"I'd wait for Donnelly and Stobbs if I were you," said Nelligan.

"Nelligan, one of the small blessings life has bestowed on me is that I am not you."

"Suit yourself," said Nelligan. He heaved himself out of his comfortable chair. "Anyone want coffee? I'll get it."

"That's real nice of you, Detective Nelligan. No."

"Art?"

"Get lost, Nelligan." The detective shrugged, picked up his coffee mug and walked out into the hall toward the nurses station. As he left the room, the ICU nurse entered it, pushing a medicine cart ahead of her. Danko stood square in her path, looking at her perfect face. He might be a Russian Communist cop, thought Ridzik, but he's a Russian Communist *male* cop, and Art couldn't fault him on his taste in women. The nurse was everything nurses were supposed to be: tall, blond, perfect teeth in a model's full-lipped mouth. Danko stood aside and she pushed the cart toward the corridor, giving Ridzik, Danko, and the uniform a nice view of her provocative rear.

Ridzik ran his hand through his hair. "Are you kidding me?" His eyes never left the nurse's ass. "Check that out. I knew I shoulda been a doctor." With a last lingering look, his eyes followed the nurse down the corridor, and then he trailed Danko into the Intensive Care ward.

Tatamovitch looked terrible. His lips were an unhealthy blue-gray, and his face was too red to be natural. There were tubes running into both arms and another set snaked across his face into his nose. Ridzik shrugged. That was the kind of thing you had to expect if you got seriously shot. The life-support systems made no noise at all, nothing like the way they do in the movies, Ridzik thought, with all their squeaks and beeps.

He stood over the stricken man. "Hey, buddy, shithead, time to talk."

Tatamovitch's eyes were half-open, but he gave no sign of having understood or even heard Ridzik's words.

"You talk to him, you speak the language."

Danko leaned over the bed. "We want to talk to you," he said clearly and slowly in Russian.

There was no response. Ridzik doubted that a man, no matter how tough, in Tatamovitch's condition had the constitution to fight hard enough to keep his mouth shut. Maybe he wasn't fully awake. Ridzik poked him with a blunt finger.

"Come on, scumbag, don't play dead." Something made Ridzik lean closer. He hooked up one eyelid, just in time to see one of Tatamovitch's dead, unseeing eyes slide back into its orbit.

"Sonovabitch _is_ dead."

Danko swore loudly in Russian. "The nurse!"

The nurse was making her way down the corridor, not attracting any more attention than an admiring glance or two from orderlies and doctors. She looked as if she belonged there. Spotless uniform, perfectly folded nurse's hat—why should anyone be suspicious? But she was moving quickly, as if she were in a hurry, pushing the medicine cart ahead of her. The two men in the anteroom of the ICU had obviously been cops. She had, at best, three minutes to get out of the hospital and into the waiting car. One minute had elapsed.

Way back down the hallway, she heard some commotion, someone shouting. People were stopping and looking back, but she kept on going as if not having heard Ridzik's voice. She turned left into another wide corridor. At its midpoint was an emergency exit. If she could reach that, she would be okay.

But Ridzik and Danko were running hard. "Stop her!" yelled Ridzik. "Stop her, goddamm it! Police!" The two cops were pounding down the corridor now.

People were flattening themselves against walls to give them free passage. But just as they were passing one of the elevators, the doors opened and two orderlies wheeled a gurney right into their path. It blocked Danko's path. He slammed into it and fell, skidding across the slick floor. Ridzik ran around it, ignoring his partner, still in hot pursuit of the nurse.

He turned the corner. "Goddamn it, lady— stop!"

The nurse fled down the hall, pushing people out of her way as she went. Ridzik wanted to pull out his gun, but there were just too many people around. The risk of hitting an innocent bystander was just too great.

The nurse was on an escalator now, heading down to the lobby. Ridzik rushed after her, pounding down the metal steps as fast as he could. He wondered where the hell Danko was? Somewhere behind him probably. Danko had been right the first time—the Russian's street moves were pathetic.

The nurse was running across the lobby. There were fewer people down here—just a receptionist and a couple of what looked like off-duty orderlies standing around.

"Stop!" yelled Ridzik pulling out his gun. "Stop or I shoot!" The nurse ignored him. Almost reluctantly, Ridzik's finger tightened on the trigger.

Out of nowhere came Cat Manzetti. She swung a canvas gym bag as hard as she could. Knocking the gun from his hand and sending Ridzik reeling. He tumbled backwards, falling into the middle of a large glass coffee table that stood in the waiting area of the lobby. The glass top shattered as Ridzik fell, leaving him lying in a pool of glass splinters. That was bad—he had a pain in his ass, literally—but Cat Manzetti shouted something which made him realize things could be worse.

"No," Cat screamed at the nurse, "don't shoot him!"

The nurse's prefectly manicured hands were filled with what appeared to be about ten pounds of Smith and Wesson. He was surprised to find that his mind seemed to have detached completely from his body. It felt as if he stared down the barrel of that gun for an hour, long enough to note that she was about to blow him away with a .22 long rifle Combat Masterpiece. He heard the roar before he felt the impact of the slug. Bye, Ridzik, he thought.

But then he was back in real time. He was still staring at the nurse and her gun, but he had also noted that a big blood blossom had burst forth on her immaculate uniform blouse. She staggered a little, but didn't drop. There was another detonation, and another carmine flower appeared on her chest.

Danko, a few yards behind Ridzik, was placing his shots carefully, trying not to kill the woman, just bring her down. But she wouldn't fall. With all the power she possessed, she raised her gun and drew a precise bead on Danko. Before she could fire, he blasted again, a killing wound this time, squarely in the heart. It slammed into her, flipping her back against the rough stucco wall. For a moment, the body seemed to be caught in that position, sagging like laundry on a clothesline. Then, as her knees buckled, she slid down the wall.

The nurse's cap she wore was pinned to her hair. It snagged on the rough surface of the wall. As she slumped, her hair became entangled in the cap and the uneven surface, her full weight tugging on it. By the time she had settled on the ground, her blond hair was askew, sliding on her head as if she had been scalped.

For Ridzik it had been a very strange couple of minutes. Ignoring the wailing of the hospital staffers who had witnessed a violent death, he stumbled to the lifeless body of the nurse. He tugged at her ash blond hair.

"What the shit! It's a guy!"

Not even that fact seemed to surprise Danko. "Joseph Baroda. Viktor's man." His eyes swept the lobby.

Cat had not hung around to see Baroda's death. She had dashed through the first door she had seen. It was the entrance to the service stairway. She was already on the ground floor, so the only thing she could do was head up.

She had already climbed a floor when she heard the door below her slam—and footsteps on the stairs. She didn't want to look behind her. She yanked at a second-floor door. It was locked. She raced up to the third floor. The door was locked. She turned and saw Danko walking up the steps towards her. He was holding his gun straight out, aimed at her face.

"Do it," she shrieked. "Go ahead! Pull the trigger!"

"You are stupid," said Danko. To her ears it sounded like a death sentence.

"I just wanted to help him," she said, tears starting into her eyes. "He told me he *needed* me."

"Viktor has ten women like you at home. All dead or in jail. He needs you now. But not for long."

"So kill me," she screamed, her voice echoing in the stairwell. "I just don't care anymore."

"Go," said Danko.

Cat opened her eyes. "Go?"

"Go," said Danko. He leveled the gun at the door lock and pulled the trigger, blowing the lock to smithereens. The detonation boomed in the stairwell. He kicked open the door and shoved Cat through it. She looked bewildered, surprised—and then grateful. She darted along the hallway, hoping she could find a way out without running into Ridzik. She had a feeling that he would not be quite so forgiving.

*   *   *

In that day alone, Ridzik had been threatened by Cleanheads, held hostage by Cleanheads, come real close to getting blown away by a blond transvestite, and had fallen through a coffee table. The needle, which seemed to be about a yard long, that a nurse at the hospital was about to stick in his ass was the final indignity. He hated needles. The nurse, a gray-haired middle-aged woman with dragon-lady glasses and a no-nonsense manner, had prepared the tetanus shot efficiently and expertly. She never smiled but somehow Ridzik got the feeling she was enjoying this.

He slowly dropped his trousers. "Listen, lady, can I have a moment to think about this? To, you know, prepare mentally for the ordeal?"

Unceremoniously she pushed him over an examining table and swabbed his ass with alcohol.

"Maybe you have a bullet I can bite on."

"Don't be such a baby," she said. She jabbed the needle into his buttock a little harder, Ridzik thought, than was strictly neccessary.

"What the hell is in that thing? Cement?"

After a while she pulled the needle out. "Now that wasn't so bad, was it?"

"It was horrible," mumbled Ridzik. He was belting up his pants when Donnelly and Stobbs showed up. They leaned against the door and stared at Ridzik as if he were the suspect in a crime.

"So?" said Donnelly. "What's the score, Sergeant?"

"Helluva night, sir," Ridzik said, gingerly lowering himself into a chair. "The Cleanheads stuck a gun in my ear. Tatamovitch is history, Danko shot a drag queen, then I got thrown through a solid-glass coffee table, and then I got a tetanus shot stuck in my rosy red ass."

"I've always enjoyed your colorful reports," said Donnelly. He was lying.

"Glad to hear that," said Ridzik. So was he.

"The transvestite," said Stobbs, "killed Tatamovitch by shooting an air bubble into a vein. Obviously he didn't want us to question him—"

Danko had come into the room now. "He didn't want *me* to question him."

"So the drag queen belongs to Viktor?" said Donnelly.

"Yes. He kills Tatamovitch because he knew I would make him talk. Better he is dead."

Donnelly nodded. "Makes sense. What a ruthless bastard, though."

Stobbs broke in, Mr. Professional. "Did you two get to the woman, the one who's supposed to be Viktor's wife? We've been trying to track her down all night."

Ridzik shot a glance at Danko. "Naaww. Couldn't find her ourselves."

Stobbs appraised Ridzik coolly. "That's funny 'cause the janitor who works at her place says that two cops came by earlier. I wonder who that could have been."

Ridzik looked him straight in the eye. "Not us."

"Interesting."

"Ain't it?"

Donnelly had departmental concerns to worry about. He turned to Danko. "Captain, tell me, where did you get the gun you used?"

"Registered in my name—Moscow Militia Headquarters."

Donnelly nodded. He shot an angry glance at Ridzik. "Sergeant Ridzik, you—"

"He did not know I had it."

Donnelly knew cops. Even these two misfits would back each other up—right up to a grand jury if they had to. Under the circumstances, he had little choice but to accept their bullshit story. But he was firm on one thing.

He thrust out his hand. "I have to ask you to surrender the weapon, Captain."

Danko drew himself up to his full height and breathed in deeply. "I say no."

Donnelly smiled. "I see Ridzik's teaching you a sense of humor." Then his eyes and his voice hardened, the smile vanished. "You give me the gun, Captain. Now." Danko hesitated. A lifetime of being conditioned to accept orders from a superior police officer kicked in automatically. "Don't fuck with me, Danko."

Reluctantly, Danko handed over his gun. Donnelly passed it to Stobbs. "Now, Ridzik."

"Yes, sir."

"I asked you to keep our friend in line. I said

I didn't want him rolling through the city like the Red Army, isn't that what I said?"

"Words to the effect, sir."

When Donnelly got mad, his voice got quieter, but there was no denying that he was real, real mad. "Don't you give me that shit, Ridzik. I said I'd make room for you on this case and I have. But as soon as you're out of my sight, we're up to our ass again in dead Russians."

"Sir, I don't think you can blame me for Tatamo—"

"Shuttup. I'll blame you for any damn thing I want. Got it?"

"Sir!" said Ridzik, as if he had just graduated from the academy.

"Good. Now I want to see your report on this. I need to see the paperwork on this whole mess and I want it by ten o'clock tomorrow morning. I want to know every move you and Danko have made."

Ridzik wasn't sure he could do that—not without compromising his investigation of Viktor Rosta. If Donnelly knew everything they had done, Ridzik's ass would be in traction. But he could tell by the look on the boss's face that he was in no mood to argue the point.

"No problem," he said finally, "I'll get right on it. Sir."

"Good." Donnelly paused at the door. "And, Danko, I would strap on a parachute if I were you. I got a couple of Russian diplomats who seem very anxious to shoot you down."

In the hall outside the examination room, Stobbs just couldn't resist reminding Donnelly of his words of earlier that day. "Departmentally I think we might have found the downside."

"Please, Stobbs." He rubbed his forehead as if to wipe away a splitting headache. "If Ridzik fucks up again, then he's outta here. He won't even be able to pull crosswalk duty."

"A bright spot in a dark day," said Stobbs.

"Where are the Russians?"

"In the waiting room, down the hall."

Stepanovitch and Moussorsky were not pleased at having been kept waiting, and they resented being kept in the dark about what was going on. Not giving out information was what they did best, and it galled them to suddenly find themselves on the wrong side of an information blackout.

Donnelly managed to be diplomacy itself. "Good evening gentlemen. What can I do for you?"

Gregor was losing some of his carefully acquired American-style cool. "We cannot locate Soviet citizen Captain Danko. We have been advised that he is working with one of your officers."

Stepanovitch broke in. "He has no authority to conduct an investigation. He was ordered to return to Moscow on the flight of this morning."

Donnelly looked apologetic. "Hate to piss on your parade, guys, but Captain Danko is a material witness in the murder of a Chicago police officer. He can't leave until we say so."

Stepanovitch was almost shouting, as if he thought that he could intimidate the two American policemen by the power of his voice alone. "By order of the Soviet Embassy, he is to leave for Moscow tomorrow morning. Failure to do so will result in a serious disciplinary charge against him. Thank you, Commander." The man's mouth snapped shut as if his lips were made of steel.

The two Soviet diplomats pushed by the two cops and walked huffily out of the room.

"Pretty mad," said Donnelly.

"You want me to bring the state department in on this?" asked Stobbs.

Donnelly looked at him as if he were crazy. "And get two more assholes involved? Forget it. They're just as bad."

In Ridzik's car, Danko did his best to think of a lead, any lead, something that could get the investigation going again. Ridzik, however, had had it.

"Give up, Danko. We're running on empty, here. No leads, pal. Nothin'. The deal is going to go down and we're batting fuckin' zero." He slapped the wheel. "Thanks to you and your 'Russian methods.'"

Danko was unmoved. "Why did you lie to Donnelly for me?"

Ridzik shrugged. "You saved my life back there with the nurse. It would have been real embarrassing to be taken down by a cross-dresser. What would my mother think." He half turned to face Danko. "But lemme tell you something, you were a real shithead later."

"I accept your thanks. Now I need a pistol."

Ridzik laughed and rolled his eyes toward heaven. "You just don't get it, do you. Look," he said, speaking real slow, "if I give you a gun, my ass is grass. Stobbs is looking to write my execution orders, and Donnelly is all ready to sign them."

"I handle Commander Donnelly."

Ridzik wasn't sure whether he should laugh or cry. "Oh yeah? He's a fucking lawn mower. Don't flatter yourself you can handle him. He's a tough, smart cop."

"He has fish."

"Yeah, well, a fish is better than some fuckin' parakeet." What the *fuck* am I talking about, he thought.

"You said there nothing wrong with a parakeet."

Ridzik shook his head. Danko sounded almost as if his feelings had been hurt.

"Okay, okay." Ridzik reached into the glove compartment of the car and hauled out a huge handgun. "Here." He gave it to Danko. "Congratulations. You now have the most powerful handgun in the world."

Danko examined the weapon and hefted it in his hand, feeling its weight. It was a fine gun, he could see and feel that. But he wasn't quite sure Ridzik was telling the truth. "Soviet Podbyrin 9.2 millimeter is world's most powerful handgun."

"Get serious, comrade. Everyone knows the Magnum .44 is the big boy on the block."

Danko snapped the cylinder back into place. "Next you will tell me America invented the telephone." Back in Moscow, that would have gotten a big laugh. All it got in Chicago was a long, unbelieving look from Ridzik. He started the engine of the car and burned rubber pulling away from the curb.

"Hard to believe," he said, shaking his head.

Chapter Nine

Mindful of the rule—a cop is never wet or hungry—Ridzik parked his car outside of an all-night diner and sprinted through the rain for the warmth and security of a corner booth in the dimly lit eatery. He was worn out, his ass hurt, and he had a stack of forms to fill out. Danko looked tired too, but he was hungry, so he just ate his cheeseburger and watched his miserable companion complain about paperwork.

Ridzik had the forms to fill out right there in front of him and he knew that if he had any hope of getting some sleep that night and making his 10:00 A.M. deadline, he was going to have to get started.

"I don't know how it is for you guys," said Ridzik, paging through the forms, "but over here in the good ole US of A, every time anything happens, and I mean anything, there's bound to be a department form to fill out."

Danko grunted and went back to his burger.

"That a fact?" said Ridzik sourly. "You got

your site report, you got your preliminary report, then you got your accident report, got a questionnaire from the coroner's office. Then there's the big one, the case report, which has got to be *typed,* in triplicate yet, which is all very funny, you know, because I don't know how to type."

He slumped back in the booth, cradling his coffee cup in his hands.

A waitress, young and pretty, wearing a tight denim miniskirt, the kind of woman who would normally have chased Art Ridzik's blues away, swung by the table with a coffee pot, offering a refill.

"And how are you two fellas doing this morning?"

"Great. I just got thrown through a coffee table and had a horse needle jabbed in my ass."

"Sorry to hear it." She reached for Ridzik's cup, but his hand whipped out and caught her by the wrist.

"Lady. I just got this coffee the perfect color. It's the only thing I got going for me."

She looked him up and down. "I can believe it," she said. Ridzik didn't like people who were so cheerful at 3:30 in the morning. He turned back to his paperwork.

"I think you are upset," said Danko. "You did not even look at her ass."

"Who are you? Joyce Brothers?"

"But you look and look at transvestite's ass."

Ridzik didn't look up. "Fuck you, Danko."

"Is that a compliment?"

Ridzik decided there and then that he preferred the Danko without a sense of humor. He decided to take a page out of the Russian's operating manual. He ignored Danko. He took out a ballpoint and started writing his preliminary, trying hard to make it look like, as far as he was concerned, Danko just wasn't there.

Danko took another gargantuan bite of his burger and watched the action in the restaurant. He examined the waitress's ass closely. It was nice.

Ridzik muttered something, sipped his coffee, and glanced at his watch.

"I admire your watch," said Danko.

"Thank you."

"Very expensive."

"Yeah."

Ridzik went back to his reports, writing steadily, pausing only to gulp his coffee. Danko broke the silence.

"Very expensive. How you can afford this?"

"What?"

"The watch. It is Rolex, yes?" The major had a Rolex watch.

"Yeah. I got it at a discount. My cousin is in the business."

"Oh."

Ridzik returned to his work. He sensed Danko leaning closer, halving the distance between them on the table.

"Fer chrissakes, Danko, $650, no tax, it's automatic and it's got day/date and is accurate to three seconds a year, or something like that, which does me a shitload of good because I'm gonna be about three days late with these reports if you don't stop bothering me."

"I was not going to ask you about watch."

"No, I know. You want to know where you can get a deal on a VCR so you can curl up in your Moscow bachelor pad and watch the Battleship Potemkin anytime you please, right?"

"I wanted to tell you that we will get Viktor, Ridzik."

Ridzik went right on writing. "Sure. I'm just getting to the part—the _Soviet Methods_ part—where the girl comes back and decides to run _Viktor_ over, instead of me."

"The key, we have the key."

"Yeah," mumbled Ridzik, "I got that in here too. We got the fucker _cornered._" He looked up sharply. "I gotta level with you, Danko. My dossier wasn't looking great, not too healthy when we met. Now that you and I been workin' together, I am gonna get busted down to crossing guard." (Ridzik was unaware that even that modest post would be closed to him.) He shook his head. "I dunno, maybe Gallagher was right, maybe I don't want to get back."

"Get back from where?"

Ridzik waved him off. "Fuck it. Forget I spoke."

Danko sat back in the booth. "I know—not my business, correct?"

"Right." Ridzik picked up his pen again, but instead of writing with it, he sort of played with it, twisting it in his fingers. "What the shit," he said finally. "Everyone else knows, might as well tell you—but don't leak it to *Pravda*."

"What happened?"

"I'm under probation at the department. I gotta watch my ass every step of the way or I'm fucked. Three months I gotta be a cross between Batman and Mother Theresa. As you can see, I haven't exactly got off to a great start." He took another gulp from his coffee cup.

"How did this happen?"

"Simple. I was six weeks into a shitty burglary surveillance. Some guy was moving big screen TVs out of a liquor warehouse on the South Side."

Danko was staring at him blankly.

"You got TV in Russia, right?"

"Two channels."

"That's great. So anyway, I'm all alone in a parked car for six weeks. Nothin' happens. The jizzhead we think is dealing sets is just dealing liquor."

"Arrest him for suspicion," suggested Danko.

"You can't do that."

"Tell him about Miranda and *then* arrest him for suspicion."

"That wouldn't work either."

"Arrest him for the liquor."

"That was legal."

"Oh."

"So on the afternoon of the forty-fourth day I get a little lonely." He shrugged. In retrospect he had to admit that it had been a pretty stupid thing to do. "So I invited my girl friend

to come and visit. So we're lying on the backseat
and I'm really teaching her how to love the
beast when the deal goes down. Not the forty-
third day, not forty-fifth day—nooo, the forty-
fourth day at about 3:45 P.M. The uniforms bust
in the front of the warehouse, fence blasts out
the back. Right past me."

"And what happened? Even in Soviet Union,
brother police would not have reported your
. . . activity."

"Even in United States, Danko. Unless the
detective sergeant in charge happens to be
Nelligan—you know Nelligan. He reports me
for dereliction. Thirty-day suspension, no pay,
three-month probation. Christ." He drained his
coffee.

"They catch the jizzhead?" asked Danko.
Jizzhead, it was a word he would have to remember and look up in his dictionary.

"Yep. Two jizzheads." Ridzik waved his empty
coffee cup at the waitress. "Yo, sweetcheeks."

The waitress, not pleased at being summoned
like that, brought the coffee pot over to the
table and topped up the cup.

"Little slow on the refill action, hon."

She put down the pot and whipped out her
order book, like a cop about to take a certain
amount of pleasure in giving a parking ticket
to a Ferrari. "Will that be all, sir?"

"I dunno. You done, Danko?"

"I would like some tea, please."

"In a glass," said Ridzik, "with lemon. Am I
right?"

Danko nodded, plainly surprised that Ridzik would know how a Russian drank his tea.

Ridzik shrugged. "I saw *Doctor Zhivago*."

The rain was falling heavy and steady as dawn broke. It seemed like days since they had last seen the Garvin Hotel. That was where Danko wanted to go and Ridzik couldn't blame him. Even Ivan the Terrible had to get some sleep. He pulled the car up at the curb.

"Might as well catch some z's," said Ridzik. "We'll be back on it in a couple of hours."

"Good."

There was no such luxury in Ridzik's immediate future. He was headed downtown hoping and praying that he could cajole one of the night-duty officers into typing his report for him.

The bleary-eyed desk clerk at the Garvin looked up sleepily when Danko pushed open the door of the hotel. The clerk had been asleep, facedown on the reception desk.

"Messages?"

The clerk yawned and stretched. From a few feet away Danko could smell his sweat and the odor of stale cigarette smoke. "Well, we're turning the water off in half an hour, in case you give a damn."

"Phone messages?"

The night clerk rooted around in the key box to Danko's room. "Oh yeah, you got a message. Some skirt. Claims it's urgent." He tossed a crumpled piece of paper at Danko. Danko grabbed the phone on the desk and immediately started dialing.

"Hey, be my guest, use the phone, as long as it's local—"

Cat answered the phone. Her voice was drawn and tired. Another player in the drama who had not slept that night. "About fuckin' time," she said.

"What do you want?"

Nervously, Cat wet her lips and tried to marshal her thoughts. There was only one way out of this—she had to sell a deal to the Russian. "Look," she said, "I can't be in the middle of this." Her fears started running away with her thoughts, trampling her carefully prepared words. "If Viktor finds out— You've got to promise me that—"

"What do you want?" Danko broke in, articulating every word carefully.

Cat took a deep breath. "I can give you Viktor if you promise me a walk when this is all over. Free and clear. No maybes, no we'll sees."

"I do not understand."

Cat's voice was hard now. "You know exactly what I mean. You get Viktor, I go free. Do you understand? Freedom."

Danko thought for a moment. This was the deal. If he didn't accept it, then he would lose the girl and, therefore, his last connection to Viktor. But yet, he could not speak for the Americans—and he could not tell this woman she would be free if she handed over Viktor. For the first time since arriving in America, Danko wished that Ridzik were there.

Nervously, Cat began to speak again. "Maybe you don't understand this, man, but I want a chance to make something right. Look—the city pays me five eighty-five an hour to teach dance to kids they hope they won't turn out junkies. Viktor paid me ten grand just to marry him. Figure it out." She wondered why she was unburdening herself to this man—yet she couldn't forget the first time they met that it was he, the Russian, she had trusted. Not the American cop.

"Listen, Viktor's going to contact me. I can find out where and when the big drug deal is going to go down and then I'll call."

Danko broke his silence. "Why would he tell you?"

"He trusts me. I'm his wife." She paused, feeling the tension within her rising to the breaking point. "Come on, Danko, don't just breathe at me."

Finally he said, "I get Viktor, you go free." He hung up hoping that he would be able to keep his word.

"Women," said the night clerk, who had been listening to every word. "Can't live with 'em. Can't shoot 'em."

If they were going to turn off the water in Danko's room, then the first thing he was going to do when he got upstairs was take a shower. He turned on the shower to give the rusty water time to get good and hot, then returned to the bedroom, stripping off his shirt as he

went. He slid the grimy curtains closed and
snapped on the light in the room.

From across the street on the roof of a tenement house, Viktor scanned the scarred exte-
rior of the Garvin Hotel. He saw Danko enter
his room, strip off his clothes and put them on
a hanger, and then disappear into the bathroom. Viktor directed the binoculars to the room
next to Danko's. An attractive young hooker,
either turning her last trick of the night or her
first of the day, was wriggling out of a clinging
dress. He could tell by the torn curtain that
she was in his old room.

"Viktor," said one of the Cleanheads huddled behind him on the roof, "what room he
in?"

"My old room, Ali."

"What he say?" asked another Cleanhead.
This one was called Jamal.

"His old room."

"So let's go take him."

Viktor had turned back to his binoculars. He
saw Danko come out of the bathroom, stand on
a chair and do something with the dusty hanging lamp in the middle of the ceiling of the
room.

"Let's move now, Viktor, man," said one of
the other Cleanheads. There were four of them,
all told.

Viktor nodded.

The night clerk just wasn't used to this much
business so early in the morning. He had already fallen asleep with his head on the desk,

when Viktor and his thugs came through the door. They made so much noise, they woke him up.

He had already said: "You guys want a room?" when he realized the noise was the sound of the phone being ripped out of the wall. "Hey—"

Viktor belted the clerk with the phone and the man went back to his preferred state, unconsciousness, though he would have quibbled a little with Viktor's methods of attaining it.

The four Cleanheads surged toward the stairs, each of them carrying their automatics.

"Let's go," said Viktor, like an infantry commander ordering his men to take a hill. On the third floor they stopped, the Cleanheads moving determinedly ahead, Viktor lagging behind just long enough to glance out of the single window on the landing of the hotel. Three stories below, the brown, turgid Chicago river flowed by.

Then he followed the Cleanheads down the hall, but didn't go to the door of his old room, as they did. He hung back, waiting.

Ali and Jamal slammed all their weight against the flimsy wood of the hotel door. As it splintered off its hinges, the hooker sat bolt upright in bed.

"Where is he?" demanded Ali.

The hooker had never seen black, bald cops, before. But she knew she had to cooperate.

"In the bathroom—but who the hell are you?"

They ignored her. Ali and one of the other Cleanheads turned their guns on the bathroom door and blasted away, pounding the thin wood with heavy slugs. The door bucked and blistered, bullets ricocheting all over the room. From within the bathroom came the sound of a strangled cry and shattering glass and tiles. The Cleanheads weren't taking any chances: they emptied both guns into the room. Finally, there was silence. Ali carved a hole in the blue clouds of cordite and pulled open the door. A two-hundred-fifty-pound man, shot to pieces, tumbled out of the trashed bathroom and fell in a heap at the Cleanheads' feet.

"Wrong guy!' said Ali.

"Shit!"

Danko had been strapping on his wristwatch when the firing started. He didn't hesitate, but picked up his gun and, running low, kicked open the door of his own room, checked the hall—clear—and ran down the corridor toward the sound of shooting. He came round the corner firing. There was one deafening roar from his heavy weapon and a fraction of a second later, after the slug had ploughed into Ali, there was one less Cleanhead in the world.

Ali's companion got it about as fast. The gun blasted twice and dropped. Two down, thought Danko—but out of how many?

There were two to go, but they both had their guns ready and they knew where Danko was and he didn't know where they were. They figured they had him cold. He was dead meat.

Jamal and his buddy jumped into the hall, springing from the open door of the hooker's room. Danko heard their footsteps, but not even he was fast enough to beat them to the draw. The first shot, however, wasn't the Cleanheads'. Danko watched surprised as a clean neat hole opened in Jamal's head. Danko knew he hadn't fired it, but right then, he didn't care who had. It gave him the time to bring his own artillery into play. The Smith and Wesson blasted twice and threw the remaining Cleanhead back against the wall, dead.

Then Danko looked around. Standing behind him, in perfect combat stance, a smoking gun in her hand, was the young hooker. She shrugged. "They killed my trick."

"How many more?"

"I dunno."

From down the hall, came the sound of breaking glass. Viktor had smashed the overhead light in Danko's room. Dead insects, dust, hair balls—and his key—had fallen to the ground. With a grim smile, he picked it up. He had his key, the deal would go down. Now all he had to do was kill Danko. It would give him as much pleasure as the deal—maybe even more.

The hooker darted back into her room, threw on a raincoat and pulled on a pair of shoes. She had decided that the only way out of this mess was to stick with the big guy. Gingerly, she followed him down the hall.

But Danko had a problem. He was sure that Viktor was in his room and the sound of breaking glass suggested that he had found the key. Therefore, Danko had to go in and take it away from him. But there were two entrances to Danko's room: one door led into the bedroom, the other opened off the corridor into the bathroom. Danko had learned all about fields of fire in the army and he knew there was a point in the corner of the bedroom where Viktor could guard both entrances. No matter which one Danko went through, Viktor had it covered. If Danko had a partner—even Ridzik—they would have to rush both entrances and hope for the best. Not even Viktor could drop them both.

Danko glanced over at the young prostitute. She was trembling like a cold puppy, and tears were beginning to wash away her mascara. She was in no condition to help. She had done her bit already, he couldn't ask her for any more than she had done.

But Viktor was in there and Danko had to go in and get him—this was the closest he had ever been to nailing his foe since that snowy day in Moscow six months before. So he had to go through one of the doors—it didn't really matter which, as long as he went through it firing.

He stood outside the bedroom door, his gun ready. He would count to three, then hit the thin wood with all his force. At the count of two, however, he was betrayed. His wristwatch, still set to Moscow time, set off the beeping alarm. The little sounds were all Viktor needed to warn him. Danko had a second to throw himself back from the door before Viktor peppered it with shots.

The hooker screamed and hit the floor. Ivan

Danko followed. No sooner had Viktor finished firing than he came through the other door, the one leading out of the bathroom. It was a bold move, one that Danko almost found himself admiring as he leveled his weapon, siting it squarely on Viktor Rosta's retreating back. Danko had always hoped to have the opportunity to kill Viktor face-to-face, but if fate was going to offer him this chance alone . . .

Fate offered him Viktor and then fate snatched him back. Just as Ivan Danko was about to blow him away, the hooker darted to her feet, suddenly anxious to get away from the scene of any more killing. A heavier finger on the trigger would have killed her, but Danko managed to hold his fire as she suddenly appeared in his line of fire.

Viktor raced along the corridor, roaring as he went. To Danko and the hooker's amazement, Rosta was barreling straight for the window.

"Holy shit!" screamed the prostitute.

"Rosta!" yelled Danko.

Vikor went head first through the window like a diver on the high board. Viktor tumbled through the air in a giant curve, tucking his legs into a fetal position. After a second of flight he hit—the brown oil surface of the Chicago river which ran along one side of the hotel.

Danko was at the window now staring at the boiling water, his gun aimed and ready to kill Viktor once and for all when he resurfaced. But he just didn't come up.

Then Danko felt a gun in his back. He turned and found he was looking into the muzzle of a .45. The man holding it looked vaguely familiar. It took a moment for Danko to place the face.

"You're gonna pay for this, Mr. Russian," said the night clerk, advancing down the hall. "You're going to pay doctor's bills and you're gonna pay to fix up this gunshot damage. You're gonna pay for new paint."

Rosta was getting away, while this well-meaning maniac held a .45 on him. Danko feinted to the man's left, trying to squeeze by in the narrow hall; the rifle barrel stopped him.

"Please," said Danko quietly, "please don't make me kill you."

The night clerk's face flushed scarlet and his eyes took on an angry, wild look. "Kill me? Kill me? I got the gun, asshole. Four years in the army." He waved the barrel under Danko's nose. "I know how to use this motherfucker."

The hooker could see that Danko was seriously considering killing the clerk—after all, he stood between him and the guy who got away, and you didn't have to know Danko to know that this displeased him. But she figured there had been enough killing here tonight.

The hooker was a pretty good actress. She decided that a case of hysterics would be in order.

"No," she screamed, her voice making both Danko and the night clerk jump out of their skin, "no! Please, don't do it!"

Danko reacted first. While the night clerk

was still staring at the hooker, Ivan Danko grabbed the rifle barrel, wrenched it free, elbowed the guy to one side, and took off down the service stairs. Maybe, maybe there was a chance that Danko could pick up Rosta's trail again. He clattered down the stairs and was gone.

The hooker's hysterics had served their purpose, so she calmed down, stowing away her emotions like a folding bed. It was time to get out of here, herself. All of this shooting was bound to have attracted every cop in Chicago.

"What the hell is going on around here?" said the night clerk. "What *is* all this Russian bullshit?"

"I don' know nothin' about it," she said. "Now if you'll excuse me . . ."

She left the night clerk rubbing his chin, standing in a pile of Cleanhead corpses, thinking about going into another line of work.

The rain was still coming down hard, but that hadn't bothered Danko. He made his way through a filthy alley to the back of the hotel. He stood on the river bank and shook his head. Viktor was gone again. As he came round the front of the building, he saw the young prostitute walking quickly away from the hotel, making for the el station on the far side of the street. She caught sight of him, too, and started walking faster.

He stopped at the steps leading up the entrance of the Garvin and watched her go. Then he turned. "Wait!" he called, and ran across the street.

The young woman had paused nervously on the sidewalk, looking up and down the street. Sirens could be heard all over the neighborhood and she had a feeling she knew which way they were headed.

Danko reached her and took her hand. "I don't understand. Why do you help?"

"Listen, mister, I gotta get outta here." The sirens were getting louder. She knew what the police would do: she could call it self-defense, the guy she dropped could turn out to be Jack the Ripper, but she would still do time. That's the way things always turned out for her.

Danko took her gently by the shoulders. "No. Talk to me."

The woman brushed some rainwater from her face. "They came into my room and blew my trick away. He had already given me fifty bucks." She shrugged. "I guess I owed him something."

"Where did you get the gun?"

"You a foreigner? You sound like one."

"Yes."

She smiled. "Mister, in this country, everybody's got a gun." She broke free. "Anyway, I'm out of here before the cops grab me. You didn't see me, okay? And I didn't see you. Nice meeting you." She started toward the stairs leading up to the elevated platform.

But Danko didn't let go of her wrist. "Wait."

"Yeah?"

"You saved my life."

She looked at him suspiciously, as if he might suddenly turn into a cop and saving his life would be classed a felony. "So?"

Danko smiled broadly, pulling her down the steps and into his strong arms. "I want to thank you." He held her tight, kissed her warmly, and then lifted her high in the air. Rosta had escaped, but somehow the thought that he, Danko, had been helped by this slim, pretty young woman, made the pain of losing once again a little easier to bear. It seemed to him that for the first time since Yuri's death, he felt glad to be alive.

The hooker suddenly felt his happiness and laughed out loud, yelling with joy in the rain. Together they had come through a life-and-death situation—they had made it.

The first police car to come around the corner was driven by Stobbs; Donnelly was in the backseat, Ridzik was in the front. All three cops saw Danko holding a half-dressed, soaking-wet woman above his head on a rain-washed Chicago street. That in itself was strange. Even stranger was the fact that Danko was laughing till the tears ran down his face.

"Ridzik," asked Donnelly, "what is Danko doing?"

"Soviet methods, sir."

Chapter Ten

A lot of people are called to the scene of a killing—paramedics, lab technicians, someone from the medical examiner's office, sometimes even an assistant DA. Every one of those showed up at the Garvin, except someone from the district attorney, which suited Donnelly just fine since he didn't feel like explaining, just then, how it was that he had four dead Cleanheads and an unknown white male, also dead, in the hotel known to have been the residence past of Viktor Rosta and the residence present of Ivan Danko. He didn't want to explain it—he *couldn't* explain it. But he could be pretty sure who had done the shooting and he could also be pretty sure where Danko had gotten a gun.

The body of the hooker's client was coming down the stairs on a stretcher and Donnelly was wondering just where he fit in, when Stobbs spoke: "All the Cleanheads—this is strange—all the Cleanheads got tickets to the ball game. White Sox."

Donnelly rubbed his eyes as if to clear them

of sleep. "Great. I can see the scoreboard at Comiskey now—"Welcome Cleanheads."

"Maybe they're all ball fans," suggested Stobbs.

Donnelly shot him an ugly look. "Oh yeah, they take a break right in the middle of what is fast turning into a war to go catch baseball fever."

"I wasn't serious, Chief," said Stobbs.

"Good."

"Well, *I'm* sure as shit serious, *Chief*," said an angry voice behind them.

They turned and saw the night clerk. He was unshaven and sweaty and his jaw had swollen up from where Viktor had cracked him with the phone. First he had Russians, then he had dead men, now he had cops.

"I'm serious about who the fuck is going to explain this to my boss. The third floor looks like Beirut. And who's gonna back me up to my boss when I say it wasn't my fault? City of Chicago? The police?"

Stobbs was good at dealing with John Q. Public. "Sir, if you'll ask one of the officers to take your report . . ."

"One of the officers bullshit, man. I heard you call this guy the chief and I wanna talk to the chief." Donnelly rolled his eyes and headed for the door.

"Hey, Chief, who the hell is going to pay for all this? I sure as fuck know it ain't going to be that Russian bastard. And lemme— Hey, man, lemme go." A uniformed cop had grabbed him by the shoulder. "Hey, Chief, and lemme tell you about that Russian. Sonovabitch stole my gun."

Donnelly wasn't listening. The night clerk, still grumbling, allowed the uniform to steer him away. "I think it's time to shake Ridzik and his Russian," said Donnelly, "and see what falls out."

"Good idea," said Stobbs.

"Where are they?"

"Outside."

"Good a place as any."

Ridzik and Danko were sitting in Donnelly's car watching as the paramedics loaded the body of the hooker's trick into the ambulance.

"So who the hell was that?"

"Innocent bystander," said Danko.

"Had to happen."

"Viktor has key," said Danko. "Now we must find what key opens or find Viktor."

"No," said Ridzik, starting up the car and putting it in reverse. "Not right now. Now we find a place where there is no Commander Donnelly or Lieutenant Stobbs." He saw both men coming through the doors of the Garvin. "Time to go, comrade."

"Hey," said Stobbs. "Isn't that your car?"

"Yeah," said Donnelly. "And isn't that—"

Stobbs was off and running. "Fuckin' Ridzik. *Hey!*"

Ridzik waved, as if he were on his way home after a routine day, and accelerated away.

Donnelly watched him go and shook his head. "I don't want Ridzik to be a cop anymore," he said to no one in particular.

*   *   *

As they drove through morning traffic, Ridzik tried to fit the pieces of the puzzle together. It seemed as if Danko was finally opening up completely—and that would make life a little easier, if not necessarily safer.

"Any chance we've spooked Viktor enough for him to just take his money and run?"

Danko shook his head. "No. He will make a deal and then go."

"Back to Russia?"

"Yes. With drugs."

"Hell, why not just stay here and do business? Join the always-growing rank of Stateside sleaze."

"Family. Viktor has family in Russia."

"Oh, that explains everything. Viktor Rosta, family man."

"They are loyal to him. He can trust them. No more dealing with the shave-headed Negroes."

"Sounds like the Mafia. I always thought it was only us pathetic capitalists who have to deal with that kind of shit." Ridzik lit a cigarette and settled behind the wheel. "Nice to know organized crime is organized everywhere."

"We have many problems. Crime families. Drugs. Black Market. Corruption."

"Jeez," said Ridzik. "You guys are beginning to start to sound like average Joes."

But that was about as far as Danko would go with the perestroijka.

"Viktor is not typical," he said.

"Naww, course not. You're all mostly a bunch

of balalaika-playing sweethearts." Needling
Danko had become second nature to Ridzik.

"You will tell commander about the key?"

"I am staying as far away as possible from
the commander, comrade, until I can give him
something that will save my sorry ass. You
think you can give an accurate description of
that key?"

Danko didn't mention the fact that he had a
copy of the serial number. "Yes."

"Good."

"Why?"

Ridzik hung a tire screeching left and gunned
the car. "Because you are going to do all the
talking."

"Why?"

Art angled the car into a bus stop, slapped
the POLICE ON CALL sign in the dash, and got
out of the car. He gestured toward a small
store. The sign over the door said: PAT'S KEYS.
LOCKSMITH. SECURITY.

"You're gonna do all the talking, because
Pat, of Pat's Keys, hates my guts."

"Why? Did you put him in prison?"

"You might say that," said Ridzik. "He's a
member of the family, sort of."

Pat Nunn did not look happy to see Ridzik,
just as Ridzik had predicted. He was a heavily
built man, the kind of guy who looked like he
was generally in a good mood, except when Art
Ridzik was around.

"Hey, Pat," said Ridzik, entering the small
store. The entire room seemed to be festooned
with thousands of keys. They were neatly hang-

ing from hundreds of hooks attached to brackets on the walls. Behind the counter were a couple of key-making machines and an entire library of manuals.

"Tell your greedy little sister to stop calling me," he said by way of greeting.

Ridzik leaned on the counter, as if he were about to order a drink. "I'll give you some friendly advice—pay your fuckin' child support. I'm here on police business."

Pat had looked beyond Ridzik to Danko. "Who's Mr. GQ?"

"My partner. We need to—"

"Look, don't give me this shit." Nunn knew a bill collector when he saw one and Danko looked like one, sort of. "I sent her a check last week, she calls yesterday and threatens to take me to court. So I figure this guy here with the cool suit is either a collector or a summons server."

"Police business, Pat, we need to trace a key."

"For real?"

"Yeah, for real."

"No summons?"

"No."

Pat Nunn seemed to relax. "The handbooks over there are alphabetical. The manuals are by manufacturer."

Danko walked to the row of volumes and carefully read the titles. He took down one or two and flipped through the pages familiarizing himself with them.

"You wanna make sure you put 'em back right? Don't mess 'em up, okay?"

Danko took the napkin with the serial number written on it out of his pocket and glanced at the number and the manufacturer. _Yale_. He took out a Yale Locks handbook and located the letter the serial number began with. _G._

Neither Ridzik nor Pat Nunn were paying any attention to him. The two former brothers-in-law couldn't help but annoy each other.

"So what happened, Art? You lock another girl friend in your patrol car? I tell you, I can't sleep nights knowing you're a cop."

Ridzik nodded, impervious to the insult. "I hear you've been inducted into the asshole hall of fame. They say it's who you know, but I'm sure you got in on raw talent. Congratulations. Many are called, but few are chosen."

"Your whole family pisses me off, Ridzik. But I don't know who pisses me off more—you or her."

"Me? What the hell did I ever do to you?"

"She said taking me to court was your idea."

Ridzik shrugged. "I'm a cop. I figure court's gotta be good for something."

Danko had found a line in the index which seemed to make sense: "G Series Keys number 1050 to 4950, see PAY LOCKS." The first time Ridzik had seen the key, he had said that it looked like it belonged to some kind of locker.

"She can take me to court if she wants, but I just don't have any more money. We both agreed on the payments, why can't she live on them?"

The pay-locks section yielded a bewildering

array of line drawings of keys; keys of every shape and size. He followed the ever-ascending serial numbers until he found his own. There was a notation under that: "See supplementary handbook B." Danko glanced over his shoulder. The two men were still paying no attention to him.

"Your May support check came back July 9, bouncing like a superball."

"Maybe I'm doing too much free work for the police department." He shot a look at Danko. "How's it going?"

"Fine," said Danko.

"Where's he from?" asked Pat Nunn, puzzled.

"He's French Canadian," Ridzik said without missing a beat.

"Oh, a Mountie."

Danko had the supplement out now, following the line of figures closely, referring to his napkin every few seconds. Like the tumblers of a safe, the numbers were beginning to fall into place.

Pat Nunn's tone had changed a little. He was trying to talk to Ridzik man to man, trying to get his support.

"Come on, Art, cut me a break. Talk to her. She listens to you."

"I don't know about that, Pat. I told her you were a weasel from the get-go. She didn't listen to me then."

Danko found what he was looking for. His key, serial number G-3291 Yale, fit a lock belonging to American Liberty Bus Line: Terminal Lockers. But there was one piece of bad news: Nationwide. He prayed it was the Chicago branch he was looking for.

"You know," Ridzik was saying pleasantly, "I even offered to pay her not to marry you."

Nunn stood up straight. "I don't have to listen to this shit. I want both of you guys the fuck out of here."

Danko pocketed the napkin.

"C'mon, Pat, wait till the guy's finished."

"I am finished."

"Good," said Pat Nunn. "So get the fuck out of here."

They settled back in the car. "You find anything?"

Danko shook his head. "No."

"So now what?"

Danko shrugged.

As they cruised aimlessly through the streets of the city, wondering what to do next, Ridzik absently noted that a city police patrol car was following them. Both of the drivers were white, so he assumed that this was not another Cleanhead now-you-see-'em-now-you-don't trick. Ridzik was being tailed by his own department and they were doing a very bad job of it—so bad, it seemed to him, that they wanted him to pick up the tail. It was like they—Stobbs, Donnelly—were building a case: officer failing to report evidence pursuant to a homicide, something like that.

They were approaching an intersection, the light wavering on the edge of a change from green to red. Fuck it, said Ridzik, and stomped the accelerator hard, meaning to shoot across the intersection and leave the uniforms trapped in traffic. But just as he gunned the engine, their siren came on and they blasted out of their lane and forced Ridzik to a halt.

The cop on the passenger side rolled down the window and smiled. "Hey, Sergeant Ridzik. Commander Donnelly's *real* anxious to see you."

The uniforms took them not to the district headquarters, but the Cook County General Hospital—the entrance ramp leading to the Medical Examiner's office, and the morgue. Ridzik felt his stomach shift. Who had Viktor iced this time?

There was a small group of police officers gathered around the stainless-steel gurney. The shapeless black body bag gave no hint of whom it contained. One of the lab attendants did the honors, unzipping the black shroud.

Cat Manzetti's face, her skin unnaturally white, her black hair plastered to her skull, appeared. Ridzik half groaned. Danko froze, stunned. He had promised her freedom in return for her help. Another score to be settled with Viktor.

"They fished her out of the river an hour ago," Stobbs said in a dry voice, as if he were lecturing a bunch of rookies. "The preliminary med-path indicates a broken neck. Strangulation, the works."

"Full autopsy," ordered Donnelly, "right away."

Danko could hear Viktor's words in the dark of the underground garage: "She was useful.

She made some of my time in this city enjoyable. Other than that, she is nothing."

"Viktor did this," he said.

Donnelly looked at him sharply. "Keep your mouth shut, Captain. You too, Ridzik." Donnelly pulled Stobbs to one side, and hissed in his ear. "If I talk to either of them right now I'll probably get a heart attack."

"Commander—"

"I mean it, okay? Shut 'em down, Stobbs. This is the end for them. I'll want to interview Danko back in my office. I want some debriefing." He shook his head slowly. "You know, I was very wrong about there being no downside." He started to walk away, but Ridzik came running to his side. He was going to have to think of something very, very brilliant this time. Donnelly didn't even have to say anything. One look at the commander's face and Art knew that the loaves and the fishes wouldn't be enough to convince this man that he deserved another chance, or even deserved to be allowed to live.

Danko's eyes had not left Cat's face. He felt sorry for her—someone had to. Viktor certainly didn't.

"She's the wife," said Stobbs.

"Yeah," said Ridzik, "the wife. Son of a bitch." And his little sister thought she had had it tough with Pat Nunn.

"You guys are in deep shit," said Stobbs.

"That's a beautiful thought," said Ridzik.

The morgue attendants started to wheel away the body. Danko watched it as if it were a train pulling out of sight. He didn't turn away until the silent steel doors swung closed. "She had no choices."

"Neither do you," said Stobbs. "Ridzik, you are riding a desk now. Starting now." Ridzik shrugged. He figured.

"Danko, you are going home. Where you belong." Danko did not move a muscle. *Not yet,* he thought.

Donnelly figured that if he could just get through the interview with the two Russian diplomats and then Danko, he might manage to pull his ravaged cardiovascular system through another day.

The slick diplomat, Moussorsky, did his best to be agreeable; Stepanovitch continued to be his usual lovable self. Both of the diplomats glanced nervously through the vines and fish tanks, into the squad room where Ridzik sat at his desk typing very slowly. Danko was seated next to the desk, staring into space. The two Russians kept on looking over there to make sure that he was still there—he could not get away again. Heat was beginning to be applied to their own heads. They had no intention of being sacrificed for Comrade Captain Ivan Danko.

"When can we take him?" asked Gregor Moussorsky.

"When I'm through with him," said Donnelly sharply. He shuffled some papers on his desk. "I'm not very happy about this. We do have our procedures, you know."

"Moscow is anxious that Captain Danko return with a full report."

"Moscow can go—" He calmed himself down. "Moscow can go through its procedures when I have gone through mine. This is still our country, comrade, and I'm still in charge of this police district."

"Captain Danko is not under your jurisdiction."

"The hell he isn't!" Donnelly was sure he could feel his blood pressure rising. "Okay . . . okay . . . when is his flight?"

"Tonight at twenty-two hundred hours," said Stepanovitch.

"Okay. I'll be done with him by then. You can have an escort to the airport, with the captain, at nine. But first I have to talk to him. You give me some time with him, then he's all yours. You have my word."

Both diplomats would have preferred to have taken Danko right then. They would take him over to the Russian Consul, have the consular doctor administer a sedative and take him to the airport on their own time, in their own way. If they could have Danko now, they wouldn't need an escort. But they knew that it was up to Donnelly to make the rules. They would have to grit their teeth and abide by the rules he made.

Ridzik was hunched over his typewriter, pecking away at the speed of about one word a month. Audrey, Donnelly's secretary, tapped him on the shoulder. "I could do that for you in about half an hour on my computer. By the way, Donnelly wants to see you."

"Sheeeit," said Ridzik. "This is it."

"Not for you, Art. Captain Danko. You're the man the man wants to see."

"Good." Danko stood.

"No. Not good," said Audrey. "If I were you, I'd wear a helmet."

Danko stood, straightened his suit and cinched the knot of his tie a little tighter, like a spit-and-polish soldier going on parade. He strode briskly to Donnelly's office.

Ridzik watched him go. "You know, Audrey, I almost envy the fuck."

"How come?"

"When he gets back home, they'll just shoot him. Or maybe the salt mines. Siberia is lovely this time of year, so they tell me. But me? There's gonna be hearings and grand juries and suspensions and the press and what-will-my-mother-say and *then* they'll shoot me." He turned back to his typing.

"Sure you don't want me to type that?"

"I'm kind of looking to draw this out, Audrey. The sooner I finish, the sooner I have to walk into the fan."

"Look on the bright side, Art. Check your messages." She tapped the phone recorder on his desk. "Maybe you won the lottery."

He typed almost another word after she left him, then flicked on the playback. There was the usual garbage:

"Hey, Ridzik, this is Sully in Cicero. We're

still waiting for the paperwork on that 560 last
week in—"

Ridzik hit the fast forward button. There
was the sound of the machine answering. It
was Pat Nunn:

"Yeah, Art, look, I forgot something. You
suck." Then came the clunk of the receiver
being slammed down.

There was a message from his laundry. His
shirts were ready.

Then there was a long pause and a breathy
voice came on. It was the voice from beyond
the grave: Cat Manzetti. Ridzik felt as if a jolt
of electricity had been shot through him.

"Gotta make this fast. Viktor's deal is going
down tonight. Comiskey Park. During the game.
Grounds keeper's locker room. Just one guy
and Viktor." He could sense the terror in her
voice. "Can't talk, it's real tight." She hung
up. When she made that call, she had been
making a deal to stay alive, a deal that didn't
pay off.

Donnelly was cool and composed. He knew,
at least he thought he knew, just how he was
going to handle Danko. Man to man, cop to
cop. He'd even do his best to pretend he was a
Russian cop—anything to get through to Danko,
to get to the bottom of this mess.

Danko stood, as he always did. Ridzik had
made it clear to him that Donnelly was now
the enemy: the commander had the power to
send him home—without Viktor. He had to
keep his guard up.

"Now," said Donnelly calmly, "here's what we're gonna do, Captain. We're gonna make you feel comfortable. We're gonna relax."

Danko hoped that didn't mean he would have to feed the fish.

"We're gonna relax, Russian style." He opened a small refrigerator under his desk and pulled out a tall, full bottle of Stolichnaya, icy cold. Danko noted that it was the cheapest brand of vodka available in the Soviet Union—but Danko had drunk worse: stuff from illegal stills and once, in the army, alcohol-based cleaning fluid. He wondered though, how many Westerners had the stomach for such a raw brew. Donnelly put the bottle and two shot glasses on the desk, untwisted the metal cap and tossed it away—he had read somewhere that was a Russian gesture of . . . something; friendship, trust, he hoped. He poured two drinks and gave one to Danko. Stobbs appeared in the doorway. The lieutenant waved away the offered bottle.

Donnelly picked up his glass and played with it. He would just as soon not drink it—bad for the heart—but he was prepared to do so if it meant that Danko would open up. Besides, a little drink wouldn't hurt him—not the way exploding like an A-bomb would.

"Now, pretend you are in Moscow. I'm your superior. Give me your full support."

Danko tossed off the vodka in one gulp. "I failed."

Donnelly nodded. Okay, he wants to make it confessional, rather than official. That was fine, as long as he got the facts out. Danko refilled his glass and drank again.

"You failed. And?"

Danko shrugged and drank.

"That's it?"

"Yes."

Donnelly swallowed heavily, as if he had taken too big a bite of a sandwich. Then he jumped up, grabbed the neck of the vodka bottle, and hurled it against one of the walls. The bottle exploded, showering the room with vodka —the liquor rained into a couple of fish tanks. The inhabitants swam quickly to the waterline to sample the new treat. Stobbs stood rooted to the spot—he had never seen his chief lose it before—but mentally he reviewed the CPR techniques he had learned as a rookie all those years ago.

Donnelly lurched to the door like a drunk man, red in the face and panting hard.

"Ridzik!" he screamed.

For a second, there seemed to be absolute silence in the detectives room.

"Yessir!' said Ridzik, hurrying down the alley of desks and into the room. The vodka fumes were overpowering. He was hardly through the door when Donnelly let him have it with both barrels.

"Let's take a look at the body count here, Ridzik, shall we?"

"That's a really good—"

Donnelly rolled over him like a freight train. Danko sipped his drink, sorry the vodka was gone.

"There's Gallagher," yelled Donnelly, counting off on his fingers, "two Russians of the regular and cross-dressing variety, four bald black guys, a naked john—"

And a partridge in a pear tree, Ridzik would have said if he had had the balls.

"A girl found in the water with her neck broke who turns out to be Viktor's wife—not to mention all the damage to police and private property. I asked the captain here to tell me about it and he basically told me to go fuck myself with an ugly stick!" His voice had risen to a yell.

Then he stopped, drew a deep breath, and seemed to calm down. His voice was quiet, icy cool, and slow.

"But I don't think I'm going to do that. *I* think I'm gonna fuck *you*. I'm gonna say you did this without authorization."

The man had a point, Ridzik couldn't deny that.

"I am going to make you personally liable for any lawsuits or civil action."

Ridzik hated lawsuits.

"I'm going to see to it that they freeze your fucking pension and benefits."

Now, Ridzik realized, Donnelly was just shooting off his mouth. He knew that Ridzik knew that he wouldn't have been with the department long enough to qualify for pension and benefits.

"And I'm going to bring criminal charges against you for supplying a firearm to an unlicensed foreign agent."

Ooooh, Ridzik didn't like that. If you don't like civil suits, you *hate* criminal ones.

Time for the miracle. "I don't believe you'd do that, sir."

Even Stobbs had to look away. He didn't like Ridzik, but he didn't think he should make things harder on himself.

"Why the fuck not, Ridzik?"

Art Ridzik tossed the message tape to Commander Donnelly.

"I know where the deal is going down tonight." Like a magician who has just produced a car from his hat, Ridzik smiled. "We're gonna catch Viktor."

Stobbs had to admit it was very neatly done. He almost felt like applauding.

Chapter Eleven

Moving large numbers of heavily armed policemen in amongst an even larger group of
innocent civilians—even Chicago White Sox
fans—is a dangerous maneuver and the police
hate to have to do it unless it is an absolute
necessity. The prospect of a shoot-out featuring
Viktor and his Merry Band of Cleanheads ver-
sus the Chicago Police Department Heavy
Weapons Squad at Comiskey Park had a considerable downside, as Donnelly would have
put it. On the other hand, having Viktor at
liberty another day was unthinkable. It was
important to stop him and stop him good. And
soon.

Donnelly and his men, plus the backup from
the HWS, were in good shape. They knew who
they were looking for, and they knew where to
find them. The cops just had to hope that Viktor
would realize he was beat, and not try to fight
his way out of the crowded ballpark. If that
happened, Donnelly might as well go ahead
and have his heart attack, because if someone

got hurt—and he was sure someone would—and he had a healthy heart, he was sure that first the commissioner, then the mayor, and finally the press would take great big bites out of it.

He had made some meticulous plans. First, he got rid of Ridzik and Danko: Ridzik was confined to headquarters, with a very clear idea of what would happen if he moved farther from his desk than the coffee machine; Danko was locked in and under guard in a police office. Donnelly would have liked to put him in a cell, but he foresaw diplomatic troubles on that score. Still, Nelligan would keep him quiet.

The Heavy Weapons Squad was on the upper decks, all of them dressed in maintenance uniforms, trying not to look like cops—they handled brooms like Uzis—and hoping their flak jackets didn't show. Every one of the entrances to the stadium was guarded by flak-jacketed cops in uniform. There were flak-jacketed cops on backup at the gates to the bull pen, and in the parking lot. There were cops in flak jackets in the service areas under the playing field, in the locker rooms, and in the offices. Even Donnelly and Stobbs wore flak jackets under their suits. If any of the fans had noticed, they might have thought it was flak-jacket night at the park.

Just before Stobbs and Donnelly arrived, it was about the middle of third, no score, and Donnelly did his last little bit of relaxing.

"This is going to be a winner, Stobbs," he

said, scarcely able to conceal his excitement.
"We're sitting on a major international bust
here. I just hope you mention Ridzik's help in
your report."

Stobbs laughed. "But he can't come to the
party."

"Just give him an 'atta boy,' would ya?"

Danko had put a lot of men in jail in his life,
but he had never been a prisoner himself. Not
unless you counted three years in the Soviet
Army.

He was surprised when Nelligan led him
down the hall to an office, telling him some
bullshit about how he had to sign some forms
attesting to something to do with Gallagher's
murder. Danko had submitted with ill-concealed
impatience. He wanted to go get Viktor. Nelligan ushered him into the room and said he'd
get the papers. Danko didn't sit down. He paced
the barren room. There was a desk, a telephone, a heavily gridded window looking out
onto a gritty airshaft. One wall of the room
was heavy bulletproof plastic. Through it, he
could see a similarly bare room. It dawned on
him, in that moment, that this wasn't an office; it was a prisoner interview room, a place
where criminals met with their family or lawyer, each on one side of the impenetrable
partition.

Just as he realized it, the lock in the door
turned over. Danko spun around and dived for
the door, rattling the handle. Through the

opaque glass he could see the outline of Nelligan settling down. There was the sound of a newspaper crackling open.

Just then, the phone rang. Danko snatched it up and looked through the interview partition. There was Ridzik.

"So much for the concept of fair play," he said dryly.

"I must get out," said Danko.

"Things don't look too good on that. Not until your people get here to take you to the airport."

"I must get out to get Viktor."

Ridzik groaned. "Sorry, man. Your days of chasing Viktor are over. Donnelly and the heavy weapons guys will get him. Don't worry. They're real good at what they do. They have that stadium trussed up like turkey. They're pros. He won't get away."

It was then that Danko realized he had allowed his pride to stand in the way of apprehending Viktor. He had figured out, through the location of the locker that fit the key—the key that Viktor wanted so badly—that the ballpark was just a ruse. If he had told someone, even Ridzik, then they would be able to get Viktor at the bus station. He had never dreamed that he would be held prisoner. He had been foolish. Viktor was just minutes away from paying over his money and getting his drugs—and making his escape.

"Viktor will not be at the baseball game."

Ridzik wanted to laugh, but there was something in Danko's voice that told him that the big Russian was not joking.

"What about the tape?"

"Lie."

"Lie?"

"Yes, lie."

Ridzik shook his head, remembering Cat's voice. "She died for a lie? You mean to say Viktor fed her false information and then killed her for it?"

"Yes."

"Just like that?"

"That is Viktor."

"But he *wanted* her to tell us?"

"Viktor," Danko said, as if that explained everything. In a way it did.

"How do you *know* that's what happened?"

Danko ignored him. "Get me out."

Ridzik shook his head. "You always want to hold out on me, don't ya, Danko? This time you're wrong. Everything points to the ballpark."

Danko's eyes glowed. "Get me out!"

"Hey, don't feel too bad—they shut me out too."

Danko pounded the thick plastic partition. "This is not right."

Ridzik sounded philosophical, as if getting Viktor just wasn't something that interested him anymore. He gave a "it's-just-one-of-those-things" shrugs. "I know it's not right, but no sense crying over spilt milk." Ridzik was doing the best acting of his life. "Now lemme tell you

something, Danko old pal. Don't go getting
any crazy ideas about getting out. The guy at
the door is one hell of a cop. Nelligan? You
remember. The guy who ratted on me. Don't
mess with him." He thought, *Pleeeese* mess
with him. "See you," he said, replacing the
phone. Now, he thought, let's see if old Comrade Ivan takes the bait.

As soon as Ridzik was gone, Danko vaulted
up to the dirty window. He pushed the wire
mesh as far out from the frame as he could. He
was at least nine stories off the ground. Not
even he could jump that. He peered up through
the sooty shaft. There were no pipes, ledges or
even broken bricks to act as toeholds. The only
way out would be through the bulletproof partition or the front door. Quickly he ran his
fingers over the thick shield, testing its resil-
ience with his fist. It didn't even bow under a
sharp blow. The window was set flush with the
wall. No brackets, no screws.

He looked at his watch. He had no time for a
quiet, subtle departure. He tapped the pane of
glass set in the door and watched as the outline of Nelligan moved slightly, lowering his
newspaper.

"Open the door," said Danko.

"Shuttup," Nelligan said, raising the newspaper.

"It is important."

The paper never moved. "I said shuttup."

"Please, Officer Nelligan."

"Sergeant Nelligan," Nelligan corrected.

"I am very sorry," Danko said, full of contrition. "Sergeant Nelligan, I must speak to you, it is very important."

"Cool your jets, Boris. I got my orders."

Danko mumbled something.

"What?"

Danko mumbled something in Russian.

Nelligan leaned against the glass. Danko could make out the outline of face perfectly. "Huh?"

If someone had had a speed gun on the spot where Danko's fist came through the glass, the punch probably would have clocked somewhere around fifty miles an hour. Not as fast as a Major League fastball, but more than enough to strike out Nelligan. He dropped to the floor in a puddle of broken glass.

Far down the hall, Ridzik heard the tinkle of broken glass and the unmistakable "oof" of a grown man lapsing into unconsciousness as a result of being struck smartly on the chin by a large Russian.

He looked around the deserted squad room. And then scuttled down the hall, adrenaline pumping through him. Ridzik was back in business.

And so, Viktor thought, was Viktor. He was getting dressed in his new run-down hotel room. It might as well have been the Garvin, but it wasn't. He shot a glance every so often at the TV news that was playing, while an earnest young female reporter went through the slight biography of a woman known as Cat Manzetti who had been fished out of the river that afternoon. When the chroma-key thrust a picture of the deceased out toward the viewer, he merely glanced at it, hardly putting the face together with the woman he had made love with for hours, the woman he had married, trusted, set up, and killed. He had not been bragging when he told Danko that she meant nothing.

He picked up the half of the hundred-dollar bill—Cat had risked her life for it—kissed it lightly, and slipped it into his jacket pocket. Then he picked up his 9mm Beretta, checked that the fifteen-shot clip was full, and slid it into his shoulder holster. The weight felt reassuring. But he needed a little extra protection. He shot back the sleeve of his jacket and locked his sleeve gun in its place. He twisted the stubby silencer into place, checked the magazine, and carefully pulled his sleeve down again. It was the same gun that had killed Yuri—but the silencer was a nice addition he had been able to get from his good friends the Cleanheads. Good friends he would not need after tonight. In a few hours he would be gone and it would be up to them to bear the wrath of the Chicago police. Viktor was tired of them, tired of their politics. He was tired of America. He wanted to go home. Home to his family.

Cat Manzetti's picture was still on the screen. It was not a flattering likeness—it was probably a photo taken from a passport or driver's license. ". . . sources within the Chicago Police Department are saying unofficially tonight that

Manzetti's murder is probably linked to an escalating drug war which—" Cat's face vanished in an explosion as the TV tube shattered. Viktor blew the smoke off the sleeve gun and slid it back into place. A few sparks flew from the set like fireworks.

He slipped the key into his pocket and examined himself in the mirror. No one could detect a weapon on him. He was ready for action.

Chapter Twelve

It was a great night for baseball. But the White Sox were losing eight–zip to Oakland going into the fifth. The crowd was small—about sixteen thousand—but they seemed to be enjoying themselves despite their team's poor performance. It was nice to sit out on a hot humid night, drink some beer, and watch the home team get shellacked. No one seemed to have noticed that there were a lot of maintenance men around, all of them bulkily dressed and sweating in the hot summer night.

Stobbs and Donnelly were high up in the upper deck, slouched in their seats, the lieutenant doing his ten-minute roundup on his walkie-talkie. No one in the stadium had seen Viktor or a Cleanhead.

"It's 9:02," said Stobbs, looking at his watch. "I thought it would have gone down by now."

Sadly, Donnelly watched a guy a few rows away guzzle down a nice cold beer. He wouldn't mind one himself—but he was on duty and it wouldn't look good to the men. "You gotta be

more than a watch, Charlie," he said to Stobbs.
"Watches are very cheap these days." He
yawned and pulled the collar of his flak jacket.
It was beginning to dawn on him that they
might have been sent on a wild-goose chase.

"We've got nothing," said Stobbs, equally dis-
gusted. "No one reports anyone in or out. No
sign of Viktor."

There was some halfhearted clapping as a
White Sox got a base on balls. Two out, but it
was something.

"What about the locker rooms?"

"Nothing in them but lockers."

The Oakland pitcher was quickly ahead of
the batter, 2 and 0.

"What about *in* the lockers?"

"Beer cans, baseballs, and pieces of clothing
the heavy weapons guys don't want to touch."

The batter fouled off a couple of pitches.

"Think he'll get a hit?" Donnelly asked.

"No. What do we do now?"

"Hit and run?" Donnelly said.

"No, I mean—"

"Fuck," said Donnelly. His major international drug bust was turning into a slow night
at the ballpark. He reassembled all the pieces:
The woman had given Ridzik the information.
She had died for it. Nobody, not even Viktor,
killed people for telling a lie to the police.
There had to be something going down here
tonight. Otherwise, Cat Manzetti would still
be alive.

"Tell 'em to hold positions," Donnelly said.

The crowd groaned as the batter was caught
looking at a fastball.

"How come no one in this city can play baseball?" Donnelly asked no one in particular.

The A's didn't score in the sixth, seventh, or eighth. Neither did the cops. The Sox got two runs—Donnelly could just imagine the sportscasters saying that they were "chipping away at that long Oakland lead." But two runs was all the chipping they did. The game ended 8–2, A's. The scoreboard exhorted the fans to drive carefully and everyone went home—except the police.

The stadium was almost empty, and the real maintenance workers were slowly rolling the tarp out onto the infield.

"I hate losing," Donnelly said evenly.

"Me too."

"I think we've been fucked." He nodded at his junior. "Okay, bring 'em in."

Stobbs raised the handset to his mouth. "We're going home, we've been fucked."

Donnelly heaved himself out of his seat. "That was a waste of time and the taxpayers' money."

"Don't worry about it. The taxpayers will never know."

"Fuckin' good thing, too."

"So now what?"

Donnelly shrugged. "There's something I don't even want to think about. But I'm the commander, I *have* to think about it."

"Are you thinking what I'm thinking?" asked Stobbs.

"Probably."

"Bad, ain't it."

"Oh yes."

They were both wondering just where the drug deal had gone down that night. And if Viktor had walked already, laughing at them.

Viktor got to the bus station just before nine. First he cruised by the dock where the buses came in, just to make sure that his connection hadn't arrived early. It hadn't. He scanned the area, pleased that passenger traffic was light that night and that the two uniformed cops he could see looked bored, hot, and tired. If Danko or the Chicago police had somehow discovered his plans, they were doing a great job of staying out of sight, and if the two uniforms he could see were only *acting* bored and unalert, then they were wasted as cops, they should be on the stage. Viktor allowed himself to relax, he was home free.

He walked over to the lunch counter, which faced the bank of lockers and the arrival gates beyond. He ordered coffee and turned on the stool to watch the area. He saw Salim coming as the numbers on the digital clock over the departure gate flipped over to nine o'clock; Abjul Elijah's man on the outside was right on time. He took the stool next to Viktor, acting as if he had never seen the Russian before in his life.

They both knew the routine. Viktor shot one last quick look around and then placed his locker key on the counter between them. Without looking down, Salim covered the key with his hand, swept it off the counter, and placed it in his pocket. When he took his hand out of his pocket, he was holding a dollar bill, which he laid on the counter.

"Give me some coffee, baby," he called to the waitress. "I'll be right back." He slipped off the stool and walked toward the bank of lockers, matching the number on the key to one of the large compartments on the lower part of the rack. The two cops were in the neighborhood, but they didn't look his way. After all, what could be more natural than some guy getting a suitcase out of a locker in a bus station? Salim took the vinyl case out, noting that it was agreeably heavy. Brother Abdul would be pleased. He walked nonchalantly toward the men's room. Viktor followed a few yards behind.

Salim was waiting as Viktor came through the swinging doors. The suitcase was resting on one of the sinks, unopened. The room was dank and sour-smelling. Viktor nodded at Salim. The Cleanhead snapped open the locks on the suitcase, lifted the top a few inches, and saw just what he wanted to see: money. He slipped out a wad of worn bills two inches thick, and fanned through them.

"Good," he said.

"Everything is okay, yes?"

Salim nodded, smiling slightly. "Everything's fine, man."

"Now tell me what I want to know."

Salim looked at his watch. "The stuff should be pulling in right now. It's on the nine-fifteen from El Paso. That's in Texas. You'll be meeting a guy, Lupo, Mexican. He'll know you. Show him your half hundred and he tells you which suitcase the shit's in."

"I can trust you?"

Salim smiled broadly. "Yeah. We want your money, but we also want you to spread that crack all over Siberia."

"I understand," said Viktor. "Good-bye." He reached out as if to shake Salim's hand. As Salim reached for it, Viktor's sleeve gun slid into his hand. It took less than a second for him to raise the lethal, silenced weapon and blast two slugs into Salim's head. There was surprisingly little blood. The man slammed back into a toilet stall, his legs buckling under him.

Viktor closed the door and slid his gun back into his sleeve. He took the suitcase and walked calmly from the men's room, confident that when Salim's body was found it would be considered just another corpse, an unsolved murder in a city that was no stranger to violence.

He returned to the street level of the bus station. The first bus he saw had CANADA marked as its destination, but beside it was another: EL PASO/ CHICAGO read the sign above the windshield. Passengers were clustered around the luggage bays, grabbing their suitcases and hustling away, or waiting for the more leisurely service of the porters. One of them was wrestling with two large aluminum suitcases, but there was no sign of their owner. Viktor was sure they were the ones.

There was a flurry of activity as the Canada-bound bus was loaded, the hatches open, the entrance door swung wide. From the crowd emerged a short dark man in a linen suit. He made straight for Viktor.

"Excuse me," he said, his accent slightly

tinged with a Spanish lilt. "Do you have change for a hundred-dollar bill?"

Viktor slid the half-note out of his pocket. "I'm sorry, I have nothing smaller than this." He deftly placed his bill in Lupo's hand, as if he had tipped a headwaiter for a good table in an expensive restaurant. Lupo peered at his bill and at the one Viktor had handed him. The hundred-dollar note had been neatly divided, splitting the serial number in two parts. There are eight digits and two letters in a bill number, a letter at the beginning of the figure, which is repeated at the end. Lupo had B 2567 and Viktor had 5093B. The numbers were the same on both sides of the banknote.

Lupo smiled and slipped Viktor two baggage claim tickets. "Your merchandise is in the silver luggage trunks." He turned as if to go, but then paused. "I have a little village down in Durango—that's Mexico—in the mountains. It's a nice place to visit."

"I'm sure it is," said Viktor, anxious to pick up his shipment and get going.

Lupo lowered his voice conspiratorially. "It's an even better place to do business, you know what I mean? Maybe next time we don't need the Americans in the middle."

Viktor nodded. "It is possible." He didn't tell the man that it was more than possible, it was likely. Now that he had ripped off the Cleanheads and killed one of their own, it was unlikely that he would ever set foot in Chicago again and he would need a new supplier in the future. He had the idea that Mexico would be an easier country to work in.

The Mexican tapped him lightly on the shoulder. "Be in touch, man." It was only a few seconds after he had gone that Viktor realized that Lupo had taken both halves of the hundred-dollar bill. He shrugged off the loss: what did a hundred dollars matter when he was set to make millions?

He gave his tickets to the porter. "Where to? Out front for a cab?"

"No," said Viktor. "On the Canada bus." He would cross the border quietly, lay low in Montreal for a few days, then move eastward, getting the drugs onto a Polish freighter, as he had already arranged in Quebec. Then would follow a long, slow, uncomfortable journey back to Russia.

He watched the porter closely as he stowed the luggage in the hold of the bus. He tipped the man well, but not so lavishly that he would remember him; Viktor allowed himself a moment to relax. The bus was due to depart in ten minutes. Then he was home free.

He walked around the back of the bus, intending to get in and settle himself in his seat. Waiting for him just a few feet from the door was Danko. He had a gun in his hand.

"You did not make it," Danko said quietly in Russian.

Viktor gave Danko a long look, trying to figure out where he had gone wrong. How could he have followed him here? He had worked out everything so perfectly, right down to the sacrificing of Cat Manzetti—a ruse he considered a stroke of genius—and yet, here Danko was, at precisely the wrong minute. He could not spot his mistake right off. No matter. There would be time enough later. Now he had to kill Danko and get away. In order to kill him, he needed a little more time. He smiled.

"You're crazy, Ivan," he said in English. "This is America. You are not the law here."

"Come with me," growled Danko, "or I will kill you here and now." He raised his pistol.

From behind them came a voice: "Back off, Captain. The Chicago police are here." It was Ridzik.

Danko's eyes blazed. "You followed me."

"You lied to me about the key," he said, but his eyes were on Viktor. It was no time to let him take advantage of the Ridzik–Danko rivalry. "The way I see it, we're even."

"I will take him back."

"No way," said Ridzik. "He killed a Chicago cop. Chicago gets him first."

The pistol swung away from Viktor and was now aimed at Ridzik's guts. Art took his eyes off Viktor and looked at the gun. Then he looked at Danko's eyes. He didn't like what he saw there: there was more than a hint that he would kill Viktor *and* Ridzik if Ridzik got in the way.

"I have orders," said Danko. It was as if the past few days, the dangers and scrapes that the two men had shared, now counted for nothing. He had his captive, he was going to shoot him or take him back.

"Orders? What? They gave you orders to shoot me back in Moscow? Get real, Danko. We're doing good here—we're taking him in—"

An old lady was muscling her bags along the side of the bus, ready to get in. They were a little too heavy for her and she stumbled under their weight, bumping into Danko as she passed. She started to apologize, saw the gun in his hand, and was sure she had walked into the middle of a mugging or worse. In a moment she paled completely. Then she screamed, a shriek so loud it drowned out the traffic noise.

It was Viktor's chance. He broke away, seizing the old lady by the shoulders and keeping her between him and Danko's lethal weapon. Danko hesitated long enough to allow Viktor the seconds he needed to dive into the bus. The door closed with a hiss.

Danko yelled a curse in Russian and dashed to the front of the bus. Ridzik could not stop him now, no one could argue with him if he shot a prisoner while trying to escape. Viktor dived into the driver's seat, wrestled with the controls, and managed to get the big, powerful engine to burst into life. There was a crunch of gears and the behemoth leaped forward. It was all Danko could do to throw himself out of the path of the charging giant.

Viktor wrenched the wheel and stood on the gas pedal, propelling the machine crazily around the parking area, making for the exit. He fought with the steering, the bus lurching from side to side, slamming into a car double-parked at the entrance to the station. The bus had sideswiped it, crushing it as if it were no more solid than an old cardboard box. The windshield shattered, glass splattering on the pavement.

The bus station was in chaos. The uniformed cops were there, waving their guns and shouting orders, but no one paid any attention to them. Customers shouted or just cringed, hugging the walls. Ridzik was going bullshit. The car Viktor had totaled was his.

A second bus bellowed into life, roared along the bay, and came to a screeching halt next to Ridzik. The door swung open. Danko was at the wheel.

"Get in," he ordered.

Ridzik dove into the bus, the door slamming shut. Danko wrenched the machine into gear and blasted off in hot pursuit, the big bus fishtailing as it made the turn out of the station loading area and into the main street.

"He has cocaine *and* money," said Danko.

Ridzik took a look at his wrecked car. "Fuck that! He just totaled my car back there. This guy is really pissing me off."

Danko drove with total concentration, but the huge bus was hard to handle. As he barreled around a corner, pulling the bus into a tight left, his left-side wheels jumped the curb and clipped a news rack, sending the metal box flying into the night air as if it were made of balsa wood.

"Jesus, Danko! For chrissake!"

The two buses pulled onto busy Michigan Avenue, both of the Russians weaving through traffic as if they were at the wheel of a Ferrari rather than a four-ton monster. There was an irate, discordant chorus of car horns as the two buses blundered through their ranks. Pedestrians saw them coming and dived for cover. Miraculously, Danko managed to get through the traffic without doing any damage. Viktor wasn't so lucky: his bus sheered an open door off a family sedan as easily as the wings come off a fly.

Viktor looked into the big mirror above his head. Danko's bus was getting bigger and bigger as it gained on him. Driving and shooting at the same time would not be good policy—he had to lose him. Without hesitation he swung the wheel violently to the left, the bus careening into a screaming sharp turn onto East Wacker Drive. Danko was moving so fast that Ridzik was sure he couldn't make the turn in pursuit. But offensive driving must have been something else Danko learned at the school in Kirov, because he hand-braked hard and threw the bus into a rubber-wrenching ninety-degree turn, and when Ridzik picked himself up off the floor of the bus he was astonished to see that they had made the turn onto Wacker Drive, still glued to the tail of Viktor's bus.

There was just one problem. They were on the wrong side of the street, heading into oncoming traffic. Ridzik could tell by the look on Danko's face that the niceties of Chicago traffic laws were not much on his mind, just then. But the prospect of a head-on did not appeal to Art Ridzik.

"Danko!" he screamed. "We're on the wrong fuckin' side of the road!" He also noticed that they were doing seventy-five miles an hour.

"Danko!"

Traffic was flying around them as the evening drivers finally came to grips with the fact that an American Liberty Lines bus was going against traffic on East Wacker Drive. Brakes squealed, horns honked—but it all went by Ridzik in a blur.

"Danko!" He grabbed the Russian by the shoulders and shook him roughly. "For Chrissake!"

"What?" said Danko.

"We're on the wrong fuckin' side of the road!"

"They will avoid us." To jump a wide traffic island in the center of the road would allow Viktor valuable seconds.

"What if they don't, you crazy—"

As if giving into a child's petulant demand, Danko suddenly wrenched the wheel, bumped up onto the divider, clipped an ornamental fountain and clambered down the other side into the right lane of traffic. He shot Ridzik a "there, satisfied?" look, and pushed the bus up over the eighty-five-mile-an-hour mark. Ridzik looked back at water geysering into the streets from the smashed fountain. This was going to be one beauty of a report he'd turn in. If he lived that long.

Viktor didn't know where he was going. The city seemed to erupt with sirens. The police were getting reports of two buses gone berserk. If Danko didn't get him, the Chicago police would. But right now, that didn't matter. If he could not escape, he would take that bastard Danko with him. Viktor's bus rocketed down the Columbus Drive ramp and hooked a right on Lower Wacker Drive. He had not traveled a hundred yards when the brights from Danko's bus appeared in his mirror. Viktor swore. Still on him. He stamped on the accelerator, weaving through traffic again.

"This has gotta stop," Ridzik said. He whipped his gun out of his holster and knelt down in front of the big windshield. Aiming the gun with one hand and trying to hold on with the other, he soon realized, was not the most efficient way to shoot at a guy driving a bus ninety miles or so an hour on a crowded, well-trafficked street. The things they didn't teach you at the police shooting range.

"Good shooting," Danko said. Ridzik hadn't fired a shot and he wondered if Danko was wishing him luck, like "good fishing," or if he was just being sarcastic. He assumed it was the latter.

"Hey, hold it steady. I'm trying to shoot a bus here."

Viktor made another turn. He zoomed up a ramp that connected with Randolph Street. He didn't see the sign at the base of the ramp, and neither did Danko—not that it would have made any difference. Ridzik saw it: WRONG WAY DO NOT ENTER.

The story of my life, he thought.

Now *both* buses were on the wrong side of the road. Viktor, like an offensive lineman, was blasting holes in the traffic, which hadn't closed when Danko's bus came charging through them a second later.

But there was no way Viktor could cut a

hole in the wall of oncoming traffic facing him
at the intersection of Dearborn. That left only
one way out. He powered the bus up onto the
curb, pedestrians scattering like tenpins. A single Chicago traffic cop thrust his whistle into
his mouth and blasted, as if a single well-
placed tweet would bring Viktor to a halt, dead
in his tracks.

Instead, it seemed to the cop that all he did
was whistle up another bus. Danko roared by
him, charging down the curb. The cop would
have blown his whistle again, but he would
have felt like a jerk.

The next obstacle Viktor faced was the gleaming red, coiled, steel mass of the Alexander
Calder artwork that stood in a wide plaza off
Dearborn. It was worth a fortune and weighed
a ton. He saw it coming just about the same
time Ridzik did.

Ridzik had no great appreciation for monu-
mental modern sculpture, but he was sure that
the art-loving Chicagoans would not appreci-
ate their world-famous work of art being demolished by two mad Russians in runaway
buses. He silently prayed that the Calder would
be spared.

Somehow, Viktor slithered around it, but
crashed through a huge glass casement in the
plaza itself. Danko was right behind him now,
following him turn for turn, twist for twist.

The two buses raced through a bewildering
maze of back alleys—Ridzik thankful that they
were at least out of traffic—ploughing through
or bouncing off parked cars. He looked back

over his shoulder and saw a long strung-out strand of twisted wreckage. It looked as if some malevolent giant had come down the quiet side streets and punched out every car on the block purely for the hell of it.

They were on Wells Street now, Danko's bus knocking down a row of parking meters as if they were daisies. The two engines of the giant buses howled at the mistreatment they were suffering, but neither stopped.

Viktor pulled a hard left, smashed through the cyclone fencing of a warehouse yard and thundered into the dark of a vast open area, a freight park near the railroad. He raced through the open area, his headlights lighting up the trail for a hundred yards in front of him. There was the snaky reflection of a set of railroad tracks and beyond that a brick wall. The only way out of the yard was the way he had come in. And that was now blocked by Danko.

Chapter Thirteen

The two buses faced each other across the wide expanse of cinder, like a bull and matador in the ring. Danko stopped his bus. A freight train crossed behind him—both buses were hedged in by train tracks—and gunned the engine, looking across the marshaling yard into the headlights that faced him. He pressed a button of the dash and the door opened.

"Get out."

"Get real."

Savagely, Danko jerked the bus into low gear, the engine growling.

"This is personal."

"What about Gallagher?"

"This is for him too."

"You can't do it for him," Ridzik said indignantly. "You're a fuckin' Russian." He jabbed the door control button. "Let's go."

Danko took his foot off the brake and gunned the engine. The rear wheels of the bus scrabbled on the loose track before finding a footing.

Then the monster surged forward, belching black smoke from its roaring exhaust.

As soon as Danko took off, Viktor was off, too. The light from the headlights of the two vehicles met and crossed like swords. But the buses thundered forward like meteors. It was a joust, the buses their chargers: Danko the white knight, Viktor the black. The buses were fueled with diesel, but the hate was driven by pride, by the determination of each man that the other would die.

Ridzik figured he was just along for the ride.

Danko was hunched over the wheel, his foot flat on the floor, his engine straining toward the metal-tearing climax. Viktor too had forgotten the drugs, the money, his brother, the Cleanheads—everything except the tournament at hand. He felt light-headed, joyful almost, that it had come to this final confrontation. He bounced in his seat, screaming in Russian and cackling with laughter.

Ridzik did not like what was going on. "At this speed we ain't going to be able to read him his rights," he yelled in Danko's ear.

"Viktor has no rights," Danko said between clenched teeth.

The buses were close now. Ridzik could see Viktor's demonic face lit by the dashboard lights.

"You know what we call this?" yelled Art. "We call this chicken. But I don't think you're supposed to play it with buses."

"This is not a game!" screamed Danko.

Ridzik felt he was close enough to Viktor now to smell him. "No shit!"

The two buses were on a collision course, blistering forward, like two bullets aimed at the same target. Danko and Viktor, hunter and hunted, had crystallized a lifetime's worth of hatred and rivalry down into these few seconds. Both men were completely captured by the moment, the pure confrontation.

Ridzik was not. He was standing over Danko, watching as every split second brought the two screaming buses closer together. "Okay," he said like a coach, "get ready to swerve . . . get ready . . . "

But Danko didn't hear him. He was not even aware that Ridzik was there. Art Ridzik, Chicago born and bred, suddenly realized that these two crazy motherfuckers were going to kill each other, with American buses, in an American freight yard, with an American cop an incidental casualty. He was now nothing more than a bit player in some weird Russian revenge fantasy.

"You crazy fuckers!" he screamed, ready, in that moment, to kill them both. This was not the way he had planned to die. A life force as powerful as their death wishes surged through him. He clawed at Danko's arms locked rigid on the wheel. He threw his entire weight behind his desire to live, twisting the steering inch by inch from Danko's death grip. A second before impact he managed to get the roaring, screaming bus a few inches off course, missing Viktor's bus by a hair. But the bus itself had taken on a life of its own. As if worn out by the abuse it had suffered, it gave up its spirit, flipping onto its side as if to die. But the speed that had carried it was too great. The huge vehicle flipped once and then turned again, and then a third time, with Danko and Ridzik being tossed within like rats in a drum.

Viktor roared with triumph as he watched in his rearview mirror. Danko's bruised and shattered bus had come to a halt as the first few licks of flame from the ruptured fuel tank were beginning to curve around the stricken vehicle. Then, to his horror, a fist broke through the window, Danko's fist, crackling the glass. Danko climbed out of the bus, dragging Ridzik behind him.

He dumped the Chicago cop on the ground. Danko's face and hands were raw from cuts and bruises, but beneath the gore he was white with anger. He seethed, feeling the hot anger of failure yet again.

"Durak!" he screamed at Ridzik. *"Durak!"*

"The fuck does *durak* mean, asshole?" Ridzik asked, enjoying the sensation of still being alive.

"Idiot!"

It seemed to Art Ridzik that it had been his swift and sure leadership that had saved them both from certain death. He didn't think that was the kind of thing that should be rewarded with being called a *durak*.

"You would have killed us, you stupid mother-fucker!"

This American would never understand. "And Viktor too! *Durak!*"

But Viktor wasn't watching where he was going. As he crossed the railroad track, a double diesel engine doing freight duty that night came round the curve of the track slamming into the bus. The engine wasn't traveling all that fast—maybe twenty-five miles an hour—but there was seventy-five tons of it: bigger, stronger, and even more lethal than the bus that had almost carried Viktor to victory. The train traveled a hundred yards down the track before it managed to come to a stop. The bus had been crushed like a tin can.

There was silence in the yard. Danko and Ridzik stared at the wreckage. The diesel engine ploughed on for yards, trying to disengage itself from the scrap metal on the track.

"That's that," Ridzik said.

Danko staggered a few feet toward the bus. His own bus burned brightly behind them, casting an oil-fire glow over the yard.

Ivan Danko took his big .44 out of his ruined suit jacket and started walking toward the wreck.

"Danko," called Art. "He can't have—"

But Viktor had. Stumbling across the track, his clothes in tatters, his left arm hanging limp and broken, the Russian advanced on them. He was carrying a gun and he was going to kill Ivan Danko, Moscow Militia, if it was, literally, the last thing he ever did.

"I go alone," Danko said.

Ridzik scrambled to his feet. It seemed as if every muscle in his body had been taken out, put in a blender, and then replaced. "How do you figure you rate higher on this job than me?" he demanded.

Danko looked back at him, blood curling down the side of his face. His face glowed in the firelight. There was no doubt in Ridzik's mind that Danko would kill him if he interfered. Danko didn't bother to answer the question.

Ridzik shrugged. "I give up. This whole thing is very Russian."

Danko started walking toward his enemy, his heavy tread crushing cinder under his feet. A touch unsteadier, but no less determined, Viktor walked toward Danko. To Ridzik it looked like *High Noon* Moscow-style, a long slow gunfighter's walk.

When they were about twenty yards apart, Viktor stopped, his gun hanging loosely at his side. He watched Danko coming toward him, a sneer on his lips.

"You want me to surrender. Yes?"

Danko kept walking.

"Take me back to people's justice. Yes?"

Danko kept walking.

"You think if you have me, you will have the whole family—yes?"

They were only a few feet apart now.

"Well, I say, Fuck you!" he screamed, raising the pistol and firing. Before he had squeezed off his first shot, the first of Danko's big .44 slugs tore into his chest. Ivan held the roaring pistol rock-hard and steady, emptying the clip, six murderous shots, into Viktor Rosta's chest. The very force of the slugs seemed to keep him standing for a few seconds. When they stopped coming, he fell to the ground. There was a spastic shiver in his body for a second or two as his brain and nervous system shorted out, overloaded by the sudden and unerring violence done to his body.

Danko lowered the gun, feeling none of the expected release, just fatigue and a faint disgust. He was still standing, not having moved, when Ridzik passed him and bent over the body.

He cast a professional eye over the wounds. "I see you got him. Nice. Good grouping of your shots."

Danko shivered, as if shaking himself awake. "Thank you."

"You're welcome." He handed the warm gun to Ridzik. He would not be needing it anymore. "I think I still prefer the Soviet model."

Ridzik shook his head. "You got a real attitude problem, you know that, Danko?" He took the gun and walked away. He had to find a phone because he had a feeling that there were a lot of people wondering where he was just then.

Danko stood over Viktor's body. He could see that Rosta's shattered chest was rising ever so slightly as his lungs fought to hang on to the little bit of life left to him. Blood drooled from the corner of his mouth, but he managed a grim smile, a rictus of death.

"I am finished," he gasped in Russian. The words made him choke on his blood and the outline of Danko grew hazier, dimmer.

"Yes," said Danko.

With all the strength left in his body, Viktor managed to raise his right hand. The sleeve gun slid into his palm. "But so are you." He waved the barrel at Danko, or where he thought Danko was, as his heart pumped its last. Danko stared at the gun held limply in the dying man's hand.

"A dead man is a dead man," Danko said.

Viktor couldn't even muster enough strength to nod his head. Aiming the gun properly and pulling the trigger were beyond his failing powers. All he could do was smile as if remembering something pleasant that happened a long time ago. He was dead before Danko could reach down and take the gun away from him.

Chapter Fourteen

Danko and Ridzik were hustled down to the Cook County Hospital to have their cuts and bruises attended to, and it was Danko who needed more attention, which Ridzik was thankful for. The big gash on Danko's forehead needed fourteen stitches, but all Art Ridzik needed was some iodine and yet another tetanus shot. Each of the cops, though, had some explaining to do: Danko was closeted with the Soviet diplomats, Moussorsky and Stepanovitch for an hour or so, and Ridzik had to answer some questions from Donnelly. He also had a couple of questions of his own.

"So you got him? Viktor?" Donnelly said.

"Yeah, we made Russia a safer, happier place tonight."

"Good," said Donnelly, "I'm glad."

"So where's the goddam body?" Stobbs asked.

Ridzik looked at him as if the answer were obvious. "I dragged it across the county line. Let the Cicero cops find him. Saves us a week of paperwork."

"That's really good thinking, Art," Stobbs said.

But Ridzik didn't give a shit what Stobbs thought. He was more interested in Donnelly.

"I always thought you were a pretty good guy, Commander."

"I do my best," Donnelly said modestly.

"Yeah, to make things harder on me. You really hung me out to dry with Danko, didn't you? You thought I'd fuck up."

Donnelly shifted uneasily on his feet. "You're a good cop. I gave you a tough assignment. I thought you could handle it."

"Bullshit. If that deal had gone down while you were all at the ballpark ..." He waved away Donnelly. "Oh, fuck it. Hey, Stobbs, this shit should look pretty good on my probation report, right?"

Stobbs hated to admit it, but it looked like Ridzik was coming back to the force full-time. If they had demolished the Calder stabile, then there would probably have been something against him—but it had come through without a scratch. "Yeah," he said, a little subdued, "your report should look okay."

"Okay?"

"Good. Real good."

Ridzik was feeling pretty good, despite the pain in his ass. "You know, that son of a bitch is a real cop. He could work Chicago, you know, Commander, if he had the right kind of partner to show him the ropes."

Donnelly shook his head. "Danko? Forget it, Ridzik. Consider yourself lucky to be employed."

* * *

If Captain Ivan Danko was happy to be going home, or sad to be leaving Chicago, or even glad that Viktor Rosta was dead, he didn't show it. Ridzik drove him out to O'Hare, checked him in for his Aeroflot flight, and then steered him into one of the many airport bars. Ridzik was a little surprised that Danko downed half a bottle of vodka as if it were Dr. Pepper before slowing down and sipping his next couple of glassfuls. But he didn't get drunk.

A baseball game was playing on the TV set above the bar—White Sox–Tigers—and Danko kept glancing at it as if it was as incomprehensible to him as an Italian opera by Bellini.

"That's Baines," Ridzik said. "Helluva hitter."

Danko sipped his drink. "Yes."

"Hey, Danko. Think I could cut it as a plainclothes dick in Russia?" And I mean *very* plain clothes, thought Ridzik, although Danko had changed back into his uniform for the flight home. The scar on his head was a livid red, but Ridzik thought it sorta suited him.

"No."

But Ridzik could see that Danko was kidding—kidding for Danko, that is. "That's nice. That's real nice. I'm really gonna miss you too."

"Good."

Ridzik sipped his beer and watched Baines hit a clean single up the middle. "Listen— something I gotta ask you. You remember back at the bus station, when we both had Viktor and you turned your gun on me?"

"I remember."

"You weren't really gonna shoot me, were you?"

Danko just stared. Ridzik thought, Yes, he really was going to shoot me. Maybe just in the leg. But the fucker would have shot me. "Yeah. That's what I figured. I just wanted to check, you know."

Danko looked back at the ball game. "I do not understand this game."

"Baseball? You're not supposed to. It's totally American." He took a gulp of his beer. He didn't think he would mention that baseball was also totally Japanese and Cuban. "You Russians should stick with that weird knee dancing and training bears for the circus."

"They now play baseball in Soviet Union."

Somehow that sort of pissed Ridzik off. "You guys don't have a chance. It's our national pastime." He watched the game for a moment and sipped his beer. "Still, you gotta admit it would be a helluva world series."

Danko smiled. "We will win."

Ridzik laughed. "We'll see about that, comrade."

Danko put down his glass and slipped his cheap steel wristwatch off his thick wrist. "In Soviet Union," he said solemnly, as if giving a speech, "it is custom to exchange article as souvenir of friendship. I decide to give you this."

Ridzik looked at the watch, then at his own Rolex. It wasn't a fair exchange, but he figured what the hell. A watch for world peace—it seemed like a fair trade.

"That's really nice, I didn't realize you guys did that. That's very sweet." He unsnapped the steel band of the Rolex. "I want you to have my watch, too. This is a thousand-dollar piece of Western technology, a marvel. It does everything but wipe your ass."

Danko slipped the Rolex over his wrist and admired it. Ridzik was less than pleased with his gift. "This is really . . . a twenty-dollar East German watch. I can't believe you gave me this," he said with a big smile. "This is plastic, isn't it?" What the fuck. It would make a funny story in a bar some night.

"Enjoy it," said Danko. He drained his glass and then bent to pick up his suitcase.

"Bye," said Ridzik.

"Good-bye," said Danko. Then he paused. "Ridzik, we are police officers, not politicians."

"Yeah? Thank God for that. What's that suppose to mean?"

Danko smiled. "That means that it is okay for us to like each other. *Oodache cheebia. Dasvedanja.*"

Ridzik shrugged. "Sorry, my Russian. It's a little rusty."

"Goodluck and farewell." He put his arm across Ridzik's shoulder, gave him a squeeze, picked up his bag, and walked out of the bar.

"So long, you big bozo," Ridzik called after him. He watched the blue-gray uniform fade into the crowd, then sat down in front of his beer again. He watched the game, figuring that after all he had been through recently, he should take it easy for an hour or two. In the middle of the seventh inning, the alarm on Danko's—now Ridzik's watch—went off. He snapped down the stem and drained his beer.

"Time to feed the parakeet," he said to the bartender.

The man eyed him suspiciously. "Just what the hell is that supposed to mean?"

Ridzik smiled. "Mister, you would never believe me."